D1273671

okja

THE ART AND·MAKING OF THE FILM

Okja: The Art and Making of the Film
ISBN: 9781785657634

Published by Titan Books
A division of Titan Publishing Group Ltd.
144 Southwark St.
London
SE1 0UP

First edition: February 2018
10 9 8 7 6 5 4 3 2 1

To receive advance information, news, competitions, and exclusive offers online,
please sign up for the Titan newsletter on our website: www.titanbooks.com

Did you enjoy this book? We love to hear from our readers.
Please e-mail us at: readerfeedback@titanemail.com
or write to Reader Feedback at the above address.

A CIP catalogue record for this title is available from the British Library.

Printed and bound in Canada.

okja

THE ART AND MAKING OF THE FILM

SIMON WARD

TITANBOOKS

CONTENTS

CHAPTER ONE: THE CREATION OF OKJA   8

CHAPTER TWO: THE MOUNTAINS   26
   MIJA   28
   THE HOMESTEAD   30
   OKJA AND MIJA   38

CHAPTER THREE: MIRANDO CORP   48
   LUCY MIRANDO   50
   NANCY MIRANDO   54
   DR. JOHNNY WILCOX   60

CHAPTER FOUR: SEOUL   66
   MIRANDO KOREA   70
   ANIMAL LIBERATION FRONT   90
   FAREWELL SEOUL   96

CHAPTER FIVE: THE LAB   104
   ALFONSO   112

CHAPTER SIX: NEW YORK CITY   114
   SUPER PIG FESTIVAL   124

CHAPTER SEVEN: THE SLAUGHTERHOUSE   132

PEACE AND TRANQUILITY   142

ACKNOWLEDGMENTS   144

CHAPTER ONE

THE CREATION OF OKJA

"It was 2010, I was driving a car in Seoul, and I saw a huge animal in a highway underpass – it was an illusion of course – a very large animal, but with a very sad expression on its face," recalls Director Bong Joon Ho. "It sparked my curiosity about why this creature was feeling this way and how such a big creature could be shy. I started thinking about it. The size of the creature lends itself to questions about its origins, for example: the super tomato, the super salmon. They are all a big size that relates to the food industry. With products, size denotes the productability of certain things, so I started thinking about production."

So began *Okja*. A film about consumerism and friendship, about communication, nature, and inherent value versus monetized value. It takes us from the gentle, unspoilt countryside of South Korea to New York, the bulging wallet of the USA. Featuring cutting-edge CGI and an all-star cast, it is one of the

earliest original productions from streaming service Netflix – as well as being the first Netflix film to premiere at the prestigious Cannes Film Festival. It may even be the most vegetarian film ever.

Director Bong's previous movies are *Barking Dogs Never Bite*, *Memories of Murder*, *The Host*, *Mother*, and *Snowpiercer*. The first stirrings of *Okja* began after the release of *Mother*, but the film did not begin in earnest until after *Snowpiercer* – his first primarily English-language movie and first with an international cast.

"Right after *Snowpiercer* we got straight to this," explains producer Dooho Choi. "Bong took a little bit of a break, but it was interesting because we put out *Snowpiercer* in August 2013, but we struggled with getting the US version out. I started working full time on this while we were getting *Snowpiercer* out in the States. It didn't come out until June 2014, so after all that period that's when we were able to catch our breath and Bong was able to focus on the writing."

"The Zoddd concept art was critical. That was the image that I showed to the studios, to actors. It was a big part of getting people to understand what this is. Jake [Gyllenhaal] saw it. There is a daytime version and a night version, with the moonlight."

DIRECTOR BONG JOON HO

"The idea was that this was a real animal," says Director Bong. "Not some cartoon, not something made to be 'cute'."

At the center of the movie, the thing that is the heart, the driving force, and the prize, is Okja, the super pig created by the Mirando Corporation. She is a character, as much as any of the human roles in the story. Raised in peaceful seclusion in the mountains of South Korea, and with her loving companion, Mija, Okja is a living, breathing animal. But to Mirando, and to consumers who have no interest in where the food on their plate comes from, she is a product – something designed for a purpose.

From a filmmaking perspective, the purpose for which Okja was designed was to create a character whom audiences could instantly empathize with. They need to know her and her personality.

The task of realizing the beloved super pig fell to Method Studios, specifically Erik de Boer and his team of visual effects wizards. Method were already doing incredible work and wanted to move into creature animation. Erik and other artists came over from VFX house Rhythm & Hues, famous for their Oscar® winning work on *Life of Pi*. They were brought in at the very earliest stages of *Okja*.

"We first met in Los Angeles. I believe it was 2014," says Dooho Choi. "That was one of the first VFX meetings we had for *Okja*, talking to Dan Glass, he's the creative director at Method – they did fantastic work on the aquarium section of *Snowpiercer*. He contacted me one day and said, 'I'm putting together a creature pipeline in Vancouver.' It was just very fortuitous, because that's when we were talking about *Okja*."

"Okja was designed by Hee Chul Jang, the same guy who designed the monster in *The Host*. He spent almost six or seven months, based off of my own first drawing of Okja [page 8]. That was the beginning point."

DIRECTOR BONG JOON HO

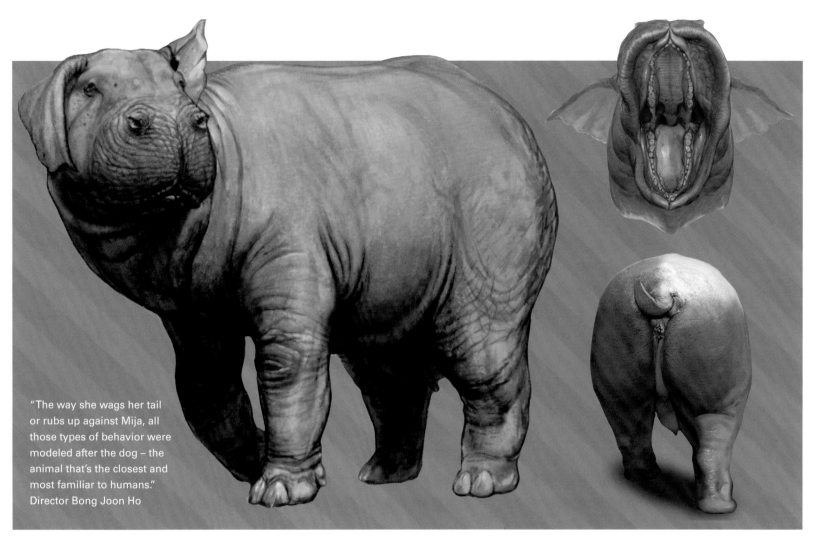

"The way she wags her tail or rubs up against Mija, all those types of behavior were modeled after the dog – the animal that's the closest and most familiar to humans."
Director Bong Joon Ho

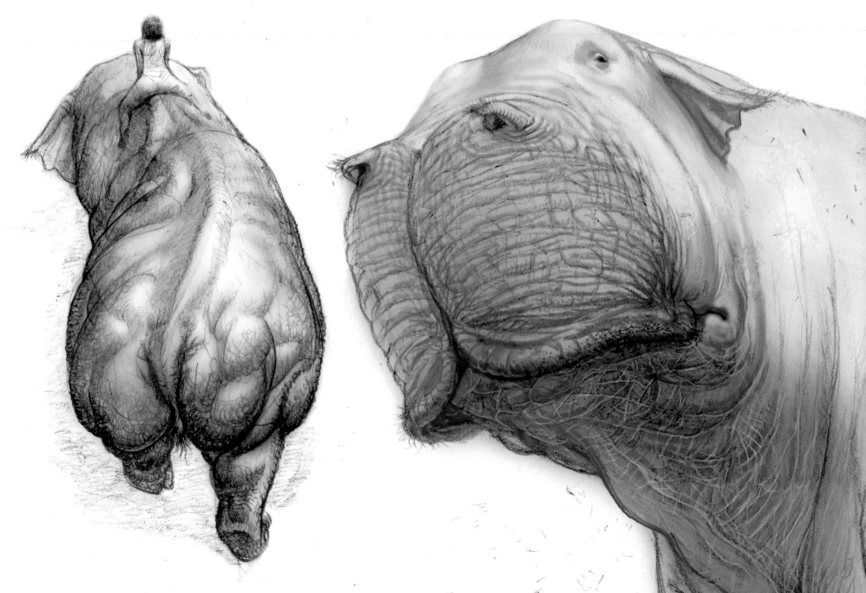

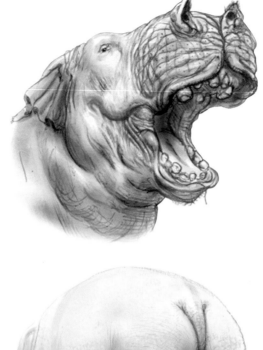

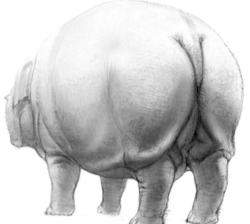

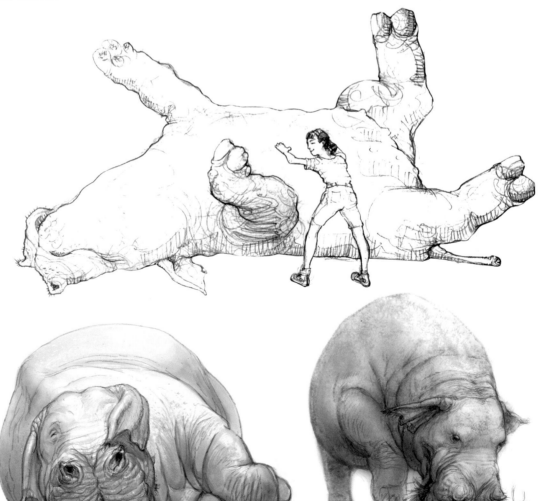

ABOVE AND RIGHT: "A meeting was held in 2014 where the project was discussed and ideas exchanged. Bong didn't have a script at that time for us to read, he just had this idea about a little girl and her huge pet pig. What we discussed was just my experience on set of working with a child actor and especially the more challenging aspect of the project, which is convincingly selling the relationship between these two and the physicality and the integration we needed to portray. We really needed to feel that there was a small girl and a pig together in Korea." Erik de Boer, VFX supervisor

RIGHT: "We've done fantasy creatures a lot of times, we have done photo-realistic animals, but then they would open their mouths and start talking. So we've always dealt with a certain amount of disbelief or something we had to overcome in selling this creature's believability. But in this case you have a fantasy creature close enough to some recognizable mammals, like a hippo, so in that sense you really have to make sure that the moment the audience sees this animal come down the hillside with Mija, that they buy into it and believe that these two really exist together." Erik de Boer, VFX supervisor

"It's such a large creature, much bigger than a cow or even a hippo, but I wanted to convey the fact that this was a very kind and gentle creature. A lot of it came from the eyes and the face. Almost sleepy, her eyes are very kind and innocent. In some creature VFX, the eyes can become larger or exaggerated and that's what makes it cartoony, so we made an effort to keep the eyes relatively small compared to the body and if you really wanted to look into her eyes you bring the camera closer to the animal instead of just exaggerating the eyes."
Director Bong Joon Ho

"Erik demonstrated what could be done with digital effects and motion with the tiger in *Life of Pi*. He feels like he was able to get the expressions in the eyes, and with Okja even more so. Along with the eyes the other attribute of Okja that is very central to this creature, is the opposite of the eye - her large butt. She's got a large butt. Huge. You wanna just touch it. Just watching the scene where she's pooping, you feel the magic, the special quality of that part of her. It's the same way that hippos poo. The same exact way. We just took that and added it to Okja."

DIRECTOR BONG JOON HO

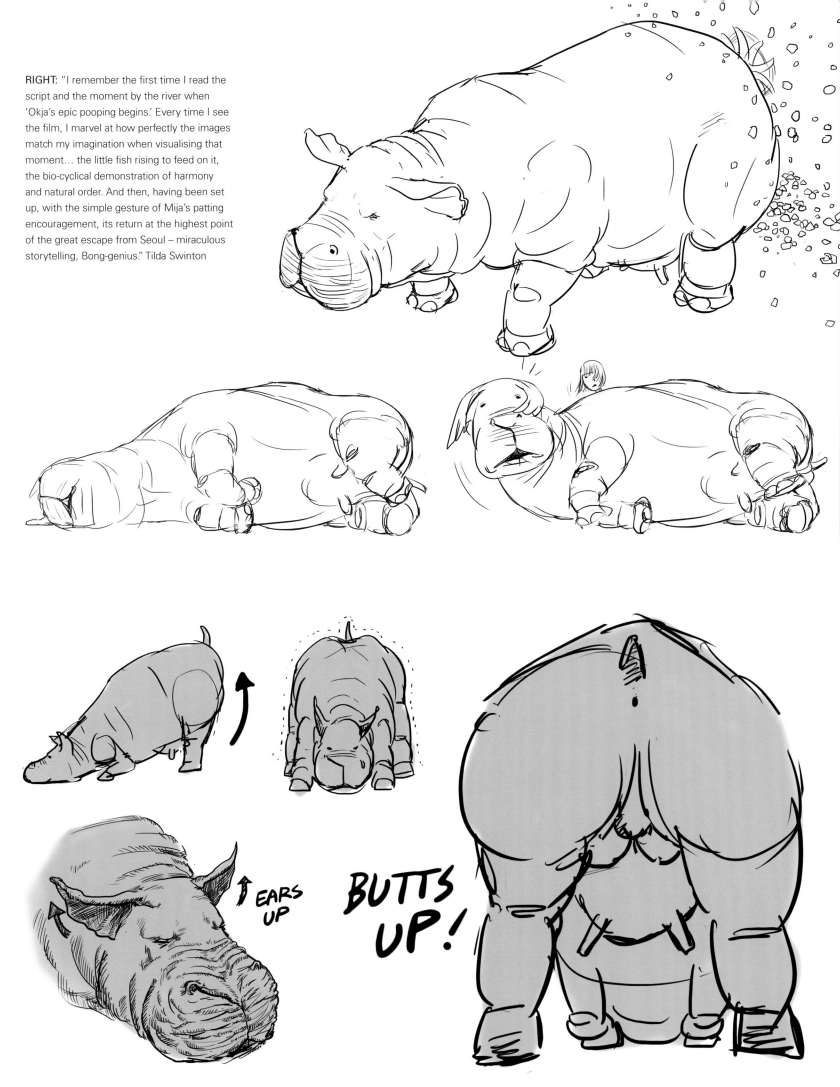

RIGHT: "I remember the first time I read the script and the moment by the river when 'Okja's epic pooping begins.' Every time I see the film, I marvel at how perfectly the images match my imagination when visualising that moment… the little fish rising to feed on it, the bio-cyclical demonstration of harmony and natural order. And then, having been set up, with the simple gesture of Mija's patting encouragement, its return at the highest point of the great escape from Seoul – miraculous storytelling, Bong-genius." Tilda Swinton

EARS UP

BUTTS UP!

THIS SPREAD: "The intimacy between Mija and Okja when they're sleeping together wasn't about how do we express this as a pig or how do we make her more pig-like, but more about showing softness. Showing that Okja is fluffy, she's like a pillow." Director Bong Joon Ho

"In terms of hitting the realism that you need, you have to look at perfect integration and a really believable contact between characters. This is something that Bong and I discussed in our initial meetings – there was no way we could be cheap about the special effects and say that Okja and Mija are together in the scene but they don't interact in a physical way, because we all have pets, and if your pet is a 6 ton piece of pork that you love and is somewhat bigger than yourself, there's no way that you're not going to lean against it, or touch it, or ride it. There has to be a physicality there, so that's really what we set out to do, which is to allow the cast, and mainly Mija, to really interact fully with Okja and not have any restrictions on that contact. Not to show off and boast what we can do with the effects, but just to make the audience believe and buy into that relationship."
Erik de Boer, VFX supervisor

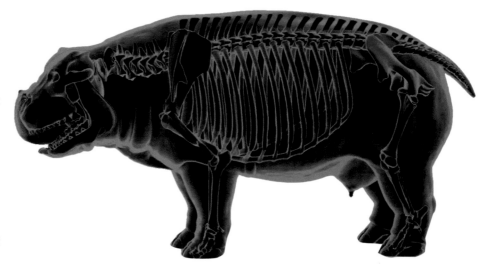

All the months of design work led to the creation of a maquette, a small model made by Hee Chul Jang and which became the starting point for the visual effects team. The maquette was sent to Erik de Boer and his team to produce a 3D scan from, and that's when the digital modeling process began.

"Our inspiration really was canine. A lot of the footage that I used personally was from a beagle that a friend of mine had named Jack. Funnily enough, the beagle, with its long ears, was proportionally a really effective reference for us in a lot of cases: the dynamics of the ear, the bounce in the body, and any locomotion stuff that we had, but also for the eyes – big round eyes that can get any treat out of you quite easily."

ERIK DE BOER, VFX SUPERVISOR

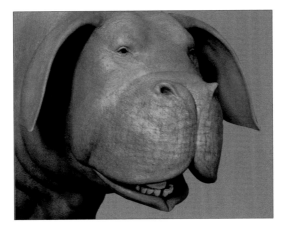

RIGHT: "The way that those eyes are modeled is anatomically correct. We actually properly reflect the light that bounces around in that eye, and those refractions are set to values that we understand from its anatomy, and that gives a very photo-realistic look. There's a lot of work that goes into modeling those eyes, and especially the skin surrounding the eyes, the lids, and the wetness of the eye." Erik de Boer, VFX supervisor

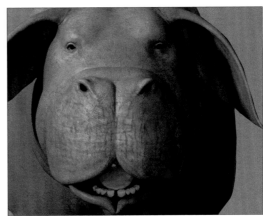

When the film began production, Erik de Boer's VFX team created a scale model puppet for the cast to interact with and for the crew to work around. Different pieces of Okja's body were made for what was needed in each shot, such as the head, detachable Velcro ears, and, of course, the butt. The puppet (or "stuffy" as it was dubbed by the crew) was created using a lightweight rubbery material that was easily transportable through the countryside and could move with realistic weight and rhythm through filmed sequences. Erik and Stephen Clee were on set every day, as Director Bong explains: "The continuity was great and the way we put the team together. Stephen was the puppeteer, he was the animator, he was the guy holding Okja's head. Then during post-production he was at Method supervising the team, so there was that nice seam of continuity between production and post-production."

That support and input from the VFX team from the earliest days and throughout production and post-production, was vital in creating a consistent character and approach. "Erik came on early and that was the idea," says producer Dooho Choi. "A smaller team for a long, sustained period was the way to go instead of, we're in post-production, let's hire 2,000 people to get all these shots done. It was really about developing the screenplay, but also about getting the design working. I remember the first motion tests that Erik did, with a car driving by and then you'd see Okja trotting by, then walking, then running, so you could analyze how well her movement matched the design and how the muscle/bone motion changed depending on her speed. That was a long time ago, but it was a key moment for Director Bong, because it was the first time he saw Okja move. Before that it was years of imagining her and drawing her."

LEFT: Stephen Clee puppeteering Okja on location and on set opposite An Seo Hyun. "We'd cover it with a grey material to reflect the different light, the different shadows, off of the environment," recalls DOP Darius Khondji. "It was very important for framing the camera, for panning the camera movement and tracking shots, to be able to figure out the size of Okja in motion."

"We decided to try and shoot everything in situ; we didn't want to shoot this plate then go away and shoot Mija on the greenscreen in a more controlled environment... We designed about 25 unique solutions, or props and set pieces, that we could use as a representation of Okja as you see her. Sometimes it was just a head, and Steve Clee would hold up the head and puppeteer it, and An would act against it. Sometimes the head was a very light version, so that we could run around with it and have the agility, but sometimes it would be a heavier version that we could bump and push and knock people with."

ERIK DE BOER, VFX SUPERVISOR

RIGHT: Photos taken at the special effects make-up house CELL where they made the practical Okja stuffies.

BELOW: An early location scout photo, before any sets had been built.

THIS PAGE: "There were a few actions that were so specific that we really had to find unique solutions for them. One of those examples is when Mija is riding the pig. Normally you would go and do that with a motion base, but this time we actually built a big pogo stick on a stand so that we could bounce Mija up and down and have a variation in the cadence, and a little bit in the angle which we were shooting her. We would have hang-time and a real percussive feel for her riding style, so you get a proper overlap with Mija, within her clothing and within her hair. You get the genuine forces applied to her legs, so that sort of physicality was taken care of." Erik de Boer, VFX supervisor

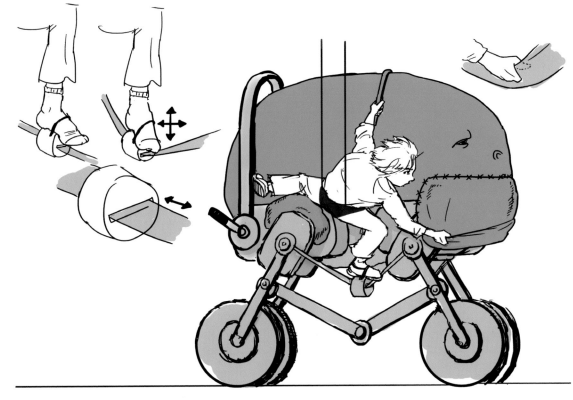

CHAPTER TWO

THE MOUNTAINS

After a breathless prologue featuring the excitement and spectacle of the 'super pig product launch', we are swiftly transported to the mountains of South Korea where we meet Mija and her beloved Okja. They spend their days playing in the lakes and valleys and gathering food from the forest.

Moving through the lush greenery of South Korea is a breath of fresh air. The stillness and lack of musical score gently settles over the viewer. There is only the ambient noise of nature. It is idyllic.

The largest amount of time on location was spent shooting in South Korea, which also doubled in some instances for the US. Once the production left South Korea, the remainder of the movie shot mostly in sequence.

Director of photography Darius Khondji joined the project early, enabling him to understand the world of *Okja* as it was still being built. It was his first time working with Director Bong.

"I came onboard the project through my color timer, Yvan Lucas," explains Khondji. "Yvan had color-corrected most of my movies and he had worked with Director Bong on *Snowpiercer*. He asked if he could pass on my contact details to Director Bong and Dooho Choi, his producer. I said yes, of course. I was familiar with his work as I'd seen *The Host* and really loved it."

The conversations about pace, mood, and look would come later. To start, they discussed the themes and meanings in *Okja*, and it was this that Khondji responded to.

"I was brought in in the early days of the project. The way he told me about it, before I had even read the script, I felt the presence of something. I felt it was going to be a very important movie. Not only a tale, but a tale that would really count in people's minds. I was very drawn to it. I needed to do this film."

MIJA

AN SEO HYUN

"A small girl carefully climbs down the hill, a straw sack over her shoulder, her face a mix of street-smart stubbornness and innocence."

THE HOMESTEAD

RIGHT: Mija's house where she lives with her grandfather Hee Bong - her parents having passed away. Okja stays in an outbuilding just about large enough to keep her. Both Mija and Okja spend their nights in there, curled up together.

BELOW: Artwork showing the relationship of Okja to the outbuildings. The house was designed by Lee Ha Jun and the production team built it from scratch.

"The beginning of the movie was very still. I imagined it like the beginning of a Kurosawa or Kenji Mizoguchi film. He's a very important director for me and Director Bong; we love his films very much."

DARIUS KHONDJI, DOP

BELOW: Concept art, detailing the path taken by Dr. Johnny and the Mirando team to Mija and Okja's simple home. It exists harmoniously with nature – no other buildings, cities, villages, or even people within sight.

"I got really deeply emotionally involved with the story, with Korea, with the people there and the nature. It had a very strong effect on me."

DARIUS KHONDJI, DOP

"I thought the beginning of *Okja* should be very calm and very peaceful, very beautiful; all nature. The camera should not move and it should not distract. To contrast with what's going to happen in the rest of the story, I thought the framing of the film should be very still and when the camera moves it should be a very slow pan or very slow track following them in nature. Everything should be like in water: very slow and beautiful and still."

DARIUS KHONDJI, DOP

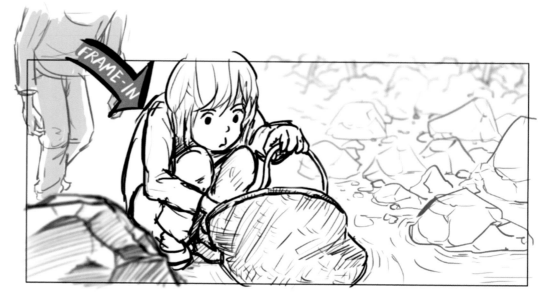

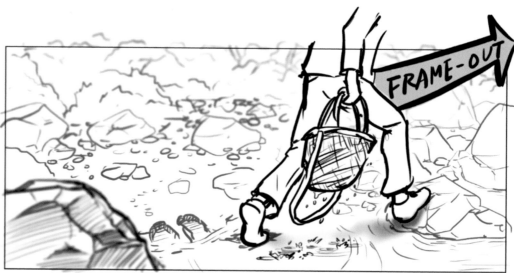

RIGHT: Storyboard sequence illustrating Mija picking fruit by the river.

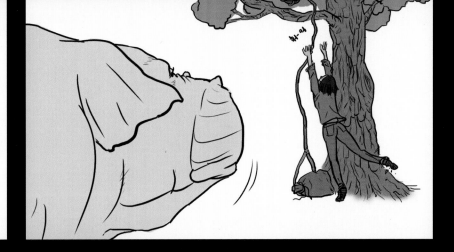

THIS PAGE: Storyboards showing an abandoned sequence. Here Okja sees and understands Mija using a rudimentary pulley to hide her sack in a tree, foreshadowing the cliff rescue.

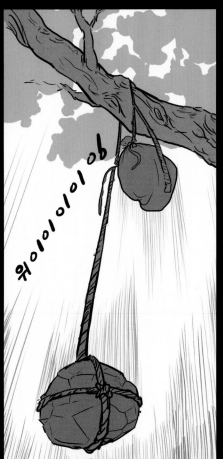

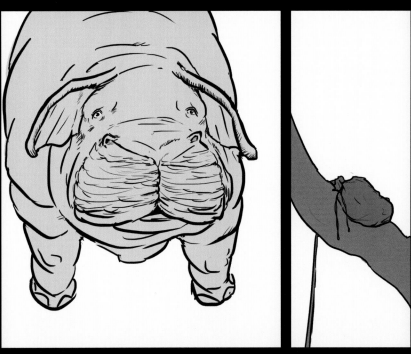

THIS SPREAD: "That was challenging work. Although there was water, on the day when we shot those plates we had to remove that completely in order to add the splashing and interaction of Okja herself - even on the simple, short breaks where she turns around and walks away. The drinking interaction is actually puppeteered by Stephen Clee. Steve is lying there and disturbing the water with his hands to get the right patterning to simulate on-set drinking. But then when she turns round and walks away we had to remove all that water and replace it with CGI water, so that we're properly brushing through the water and getting the right spray and foam flicking off her legs."
Erik de Boer, VFX supervisor

OKJA AND MIJA

THIS PAGE: On their way back home after a long day taking it easy, Mija slips down a cliff drop, desperately hanging onto a rope with Okja at the other end. It is Okja who finds a way to save her.

THIS PAGE: "There were a few complicated sequences. The one that comes to mind immediately was the shooting of the cliff; all the cliff stunts of Mija hanging in the air and Okja falling into the forest. All of this technically, including the lighting, was very complicated and challenging. We were very well supported by all the pre-viz, because Director Bong had done extremely precise pre-viz and was very well supported by Erik for the VFX." Darius Khondji, DOP

BELOW: Sketching out how to shoot the cliff sequence, complete with bluescreens to add in the great valley drop around them. "Bong had picked a cliff in Korea that he really liked, but for safety and scheduling reasons we never went there to shoot," remembers Erik de Boer. "So instead, we moved that shoot to Vancouver where we shot the bluescreen work for Mija sliding down and hanging off the rope. We really didn't have the right material, so we ended up designing our way around it a little bit, and turning the whole cliff-face into a rock-face, which allowed us to set the steepness and the look in post-production. A lot of those shots are actually CGI: at the bottom of the valley, a full CGI cliff-face, and then a full CGI slope at the top."

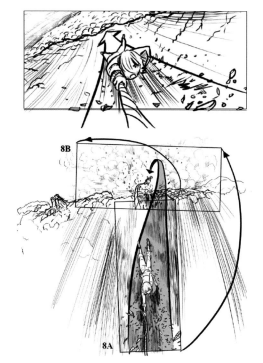

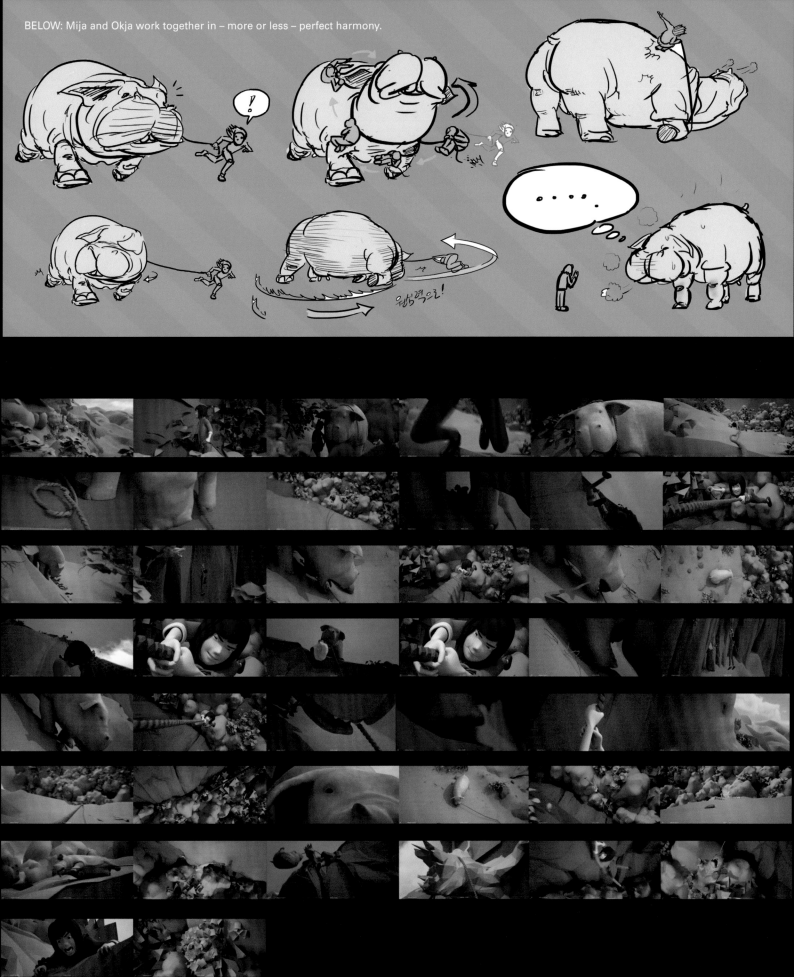

BELOW: Mija and Okja work together in – more or less – perfect harmony.

"Director Bong actually camped down inside that canyon. He didn't want to take the high trek back up to the cars and drive all the way out, so he spent a few nights camping there, which was pretty funny. On the way out we had a small model of a piglet and, somehow, when they were loading the helicopter they didn't load it carefully or they were a little nonchalant and the piglet fell out of the sling that it was being loaded in. They never found it or retrieved it, so somewhere in the Korean forest there's a piglet lying around, and someone's going to come across it one day and wonder what the hell it is." Erik de Boer, VFX supervisor

"The Korean crew were all talking with Director Bong about Okja, about the presence of Okja and the nature of Okja and how she was funny and sweet and mischievous sometimes, and the interaction with Mija. The way they were talking about Okja was very strong, very beautiful, they were talking about her as if she really existed. I was looking around at nature as they were talking and I felt she was really alive. She could be running and heading to us at any moment, coming down the hill or appearing behind some trees. It was a very strange impression. In their minds, Okja was already 3D, she was already body and soul – alive."

DARIUS KHONDJI, DOP

ABOVE LEFT: Director Bong Joon Ho with An Seo Hyun.

LEFT: Mija collects persimmons – Okja's favorite fruit. Okja notices.

ABOVE: Hee Bong (Byun Heebong) makes a gift to Mija of a golden pig, a practise, Director Bong explains, that has become outdated. "Older generations would have done that, but not so much anymore… from the grandfather's point of view he just wanted to create a little separation for Mija; she's getting older and all she does is hang out with Okja all day."

"At the beginning we just wanted to feel Mija, very peacefully, without any tricks. Just like a painting, to see the beauty of her friendship and humanity in nature. The moment she starts running then the camera starts to fire up and we released all the tension and the camera speeds up. Then we have a very fast track. We used different tricks of the trade to be able to follow Mija in action, running in the countryside. The camera, the momentum, doesn't stop again until we get back to the countryside at the end of the film."

DARIUS KHONDJI, DOP

THIS SPREAD: Artwork illustrating an alternate, unused section of Mija's flight from the forest.

RIGHT: "When Mija comes back and realizes that they've taken Okja, she runs down the hill and there's a very wide shot of her sliding down the side of the mountain. That whole sequence with the music has a very powerful effect on me for some reason." Director Bong Joon Ho

BELOW: Mija in her instantly recognizable outfit. Her trusty fanny pack or "bum bag" contains what little money she has, the golden pig given to her by Hee Bong, and a persimmon for Okja.

OPPOSITE BELOW: Storyboards by Director Bong showing Mija's desperate race down the mountain after Okja.

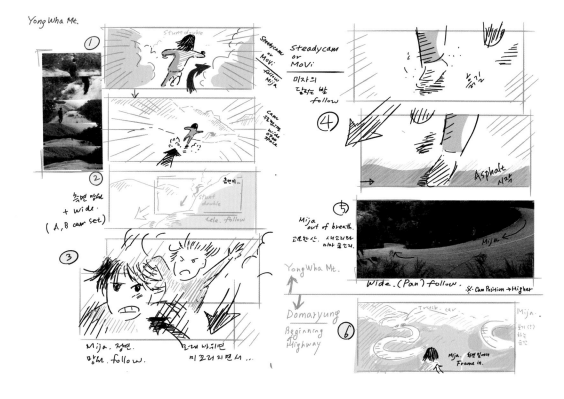

"There were some pretty exciting moments there, with some very expensive camera equipment being pushed around in little blow-up boats up the river, and very precariously perched on a tripod arm on algae-grown rock. It was an exciting few days shooting that stuff there, especially since the canyon is pretty steep, so catching the right moment of the day was very important in terms of how the lighting penetrated the forest canopy and made its way to the floor of the canyon. So that was tricky but spectacular film-making."

ERIK DE BOER, VFX SUPERVISOR

CHAPTER THREE

MIRANDO CORP

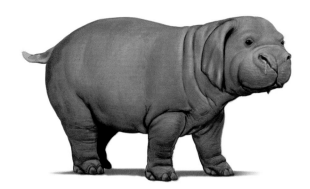

Mirando is the powerful multinational company that is the catalyst for the whole movie. In the prologue that opens the film, Lucy Mirando – the bright new face of the corporation – announces her major new initiative: in order to combat the growing population crisis and lack of food for all, Lucy claims Mirando have discovered a new breed of super pigs that will be a "revolution in the livestock industry." What Lucy announces is, of course, not the whole story.

In actuality, the super pigs have been grown in a laboratory. They are GM foods through and through, but this is not the impression Lucy wants to give of her considerate, environmentally friendly family business. As she puts it, "It's not our fault that the consumers are so paranoid about GM foods."

"Lucy's cute," says Director Bong. "You feel for her. She doesn't believe she's doing something wrong. She really thinks she's going to help the world. She believes her own lie."

The other side of Mirando, the face the public doesn't see, is Lucy's twin sister, Nancy. The glad-handing and public perception of Mirando is of no interest to her; she wants to run a business, she wants results, and if the general public wants to buy meat then she'll slaughter a pig for them.

Tilda Swinton plays both roles and delved into what both sisters mean for the film: "We liked the idea of them being, on some level, two sides of the same coin, possibly even some sort of delusion - one person. After all, when Nancy appears, Lucy leaves the scene…

"The idea of splitting a portrait gave us major scope to trawl the airwaves for actual tendencies in public figures. Several inspirations spurred us on: we were clear that however extreme we felt like being, we could never be too extreme given the range of self-promoters advocating super eco-friendly products and services out there, while making enormous amounts of money in profit, while exploiting their workers, all at the same time. However, we were not looking to involve actual mimicry of any specific person."

And so Mija has to rescue her friend from a company who is the distillation of a hypocritical 21st century corporation, dressing their greed up in jargon and quote-ready statements. The journey the two will go on is both a journey into the unknown, but simultaneously, a strange homecoming. After all, Mirando created Okja and the Super Pig Program, though the animals are bred only to be killed. They would not exist without Mirando, but they cannot live so long as Mirando continues to operate.

LUCY MIRANDO

TILDA SWINTON

"Lucy is surrounded by a makeup artist, a hair stylist, and Mirando company employees, including Lucy's senior assistant Frank Dawson. They both glance at an advertising poster framed on the wall – a photograph of a farmer gently stroking a cow's face. The slogan: The secret ingredient in our tenderloins? Tenderness."

"We were in Seoul having presented the premiere of *Snowpiercer*, and Director Bong was taking us to the airport to fly home to Scotland when he handed me a small graphic drawing on his iPad of a girl and a giant pig. That was his pitch. I was hooked."

TILDA SWINTON

THIS SPREAD: Lucy takes center stage, giving a graceful yet assured performance. In a dual role, Tilda Swinton used her physicality to clearly delineate between the two characters, which encouraged DOP Darius Khondji to change his approach. "I remember widening the camera for Tilda instead of going for a close-up," he explains. "She's so grand and she brings so much with her movements. Her body language is like a close-up. You want to capture her hands, the tip of her feet, her toes. You don't want to miss one part of her, because her whole body is like choreography for her character."

NANCY MIRANDO

THIS PAGE: Nancy – the unapproachable power dresser. She wards off contact with the permanent barriers put in place by her outfit - sunglasses, leather gloves, padded jacket. Even her neck is largely covered by a scarf. She smokes green-tipped cigarettes, while Lucy smokes pink. At one moment (the only scene the sisters share on screen) Nancy lights Lucy's cigarette with her own, a precise action Tilda Swinton described as the most challenging moment of the shoot by far.

"In *Snowpiercer* we had the opportunity, with the character of Minister Mason, the 'mild-mannered man in a suit'
politician of the original script, to make a portrait of something pretty precise: a construct, a mashup of tendencies
and posturings that we harvested from the many examples of bombastic world leaders, from Mussolini to Gaddafi, Idi
Amin to Berlusconi to Thatcher. We looked at the ways in which, very often, our leaders become framed as buffoons
in our eyes, somehow softened as clown characters that both entertain us and somehow, by being in some way
ridiculous, illicit our sympathy. This prioritizing of being entertained is, naturally, a dangerous habit in a society where
the truly exploitative power of despotic 'showmen' can be lost under the laughter-track that accompanies them."

TILDA SWINTON

ABOVE: Various designs for the Mirando branding, all accentuating the modern, fresh synthesizing of science and nature.

RIGHT: "The trademark green was brought into the design by running a ribbon up to the door in AstroTurf (fake grass) and continuing down the stairs and into the space to guide people - Mirando's version of the yellow brick road from *The Wizard of Oz*." Kevin Thompson, production designer

"Branding the identity of Mirando became one of the first design elements for the movie. Mirando is an established global conglomerate, consisting of many companies having to do with everything from food manufacturing to soap. The company is going through changes and recently has tried to update its image to an eco friendly, politically correct, health-conscious company." Kevin Thompson, production designer

BELOW: "Green was a natural choice to represent fresh, eco-conscious, and healthy. The Baobab Tree is a long-lived, ancient symbol of nature and growth. It is known as the tree of life. Because of the silhouette, we were interested in a specific type of tree, the *Adansonia grandidieri*, from Madagascar." Kevin Thompson, production designer

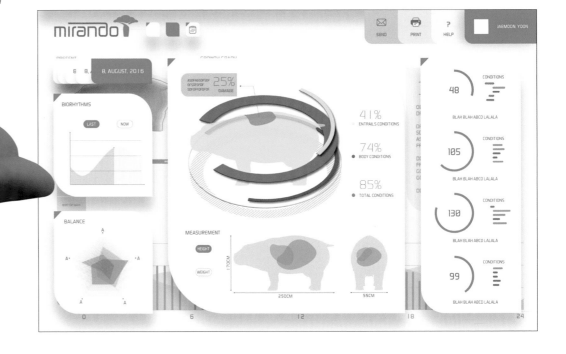

LEFT: The Yardley building in New Jersey, an old building repurposed for something new - this is Lucy Mirando's aim of bringing her company into the 21st century.

BELOW LEFT AND BELOW: Comparison between development imagery and a final film still of Lucy's speech which opens the film. The interior of the Mirando presentation was shot in Vancouver.

"The old warehouse that was used at the beginning for the announcement of the super pig competition was showing how the new chairman, Lucy, was trying to think outside of the box for the big event, by using an old processing plant of her grandfather's. The media rushes to events that are in new, fantastic spaces that they have not seen before, so this was a great corporate commercial choice for the announcement."

KEVIN THOMPSON, PRODUCTION DESIGNER

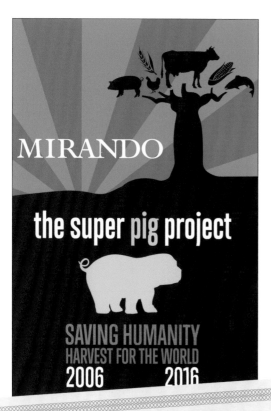

ABOVE: "This tree became the inspiration for the Mirando logo and branding for the company. We developed logos for the 10 year period that the company is represented through in the film. We started with a version that has animals and grain silhouettes as the branches, and 10 years later is the modern, simplified, yet still eco-conscious green with a nod to the original branding." Kevin Thompson, production designer

ABOVE RIGHT: Artwork that expresses everything Lucy wants her and Mirando to be perceived as: fun, successful, bright, and playful. The Super Pig Project is a 10-year plan that will culminate in a competition to see which of the original 26 super pigs will be crowned the best. "Best" in this context can be taken to mean "most appetizing."

The Super Pig™ Project

We placed 26 piglets in 26 different countries with esteemed farmers. Only one was crowned Super Pig™!

Rollover for more info

Our Super Pig™ Project Winner

Meet Okja, the crowned winner of our Super Pig Project. Raised in South Korea by esteemed Farmer, Okja will go on to feed the world!

"The world is running out of food and we're not talking about it"

– Lucy Mirando, CEO, Mirando Corporation

Follow Lucy on Twitter

DR. JOHNNY WILCOX

JAKE GYLLENHAAL

"A gorilla throws straw in Dr. Johnny's face.
Dr. Johnny laughs uproariously. Dr. Johnny lies
underneath an elephant, washing its underside.
The elephant takes a shit on Dr. Johnny's face.
Dr. Johnny shrieks with laughter."

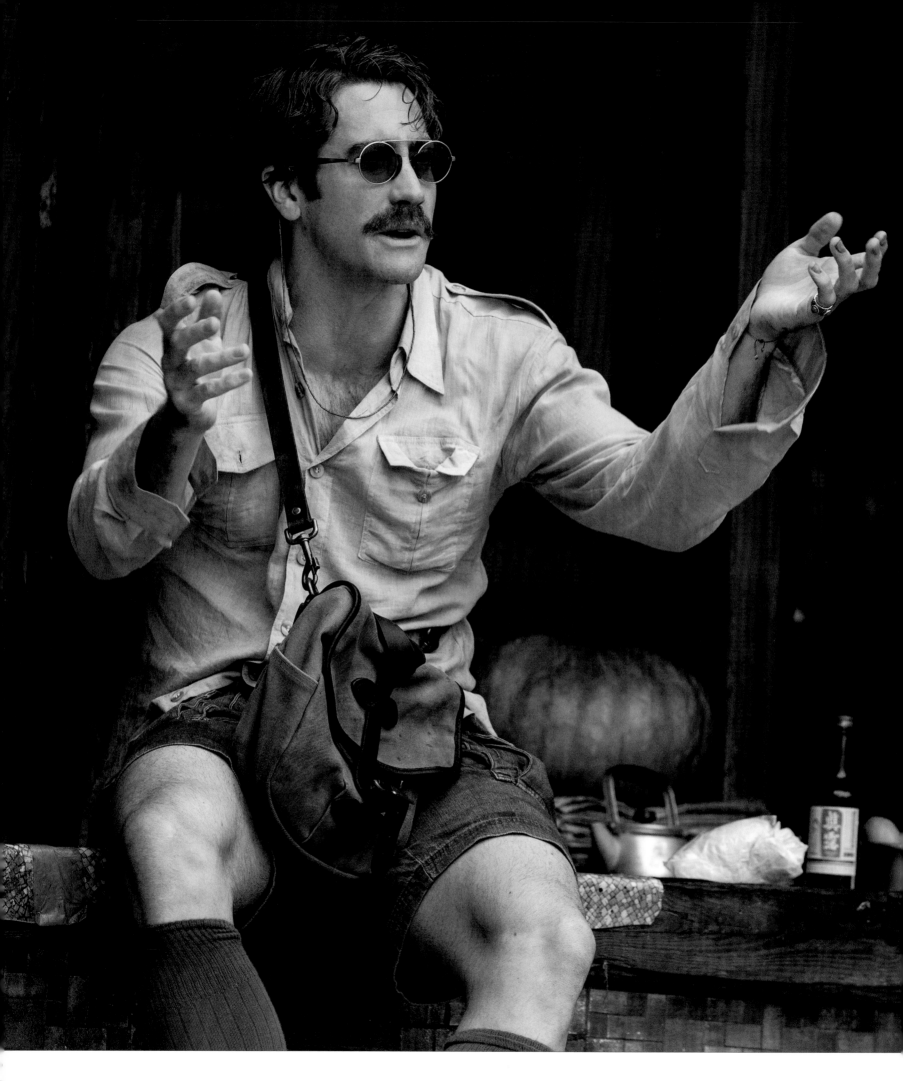

LEFT AND BELOW LEFT: "Part circus, part carnival, part corporate event, part Macy's Day parade, part ticker tape parade, the Super Pig Festival was placed in classic Downtown Manhattan, near the stock exchange. Sample sausages are thrown to the crowd by 'piglet girls' riding in farm wagons on hay bales; a giant super pig balloon floats above the band. Dr. Johnny is the master of ceremonies." Kevin Thompson, production designer

OVERLEAF: "The graphics were designed to be pop, fun, familiar, and were influenced by elements of show business mixed with the circus and vaudeville." Kevin Thompson, production designer

CHAPTER FOUR

SEOUL

Unbeknownst to Mija, the arrival in South Korea of Dr. Johnny, Mirando's ambassador, means taking Okja to the USA for the final leg of the super pig competition. Whilst Hee Bong distracts Mija and tries to soften the blow by offering her a traditional golden pig, when she returns to the homestead, Okja is gone and the tranquility of their mountain life is shattered.

She, and the camera, set off in pursuit and the race to save Okja begins. Mija arrives in Seoul and pushes her way through the hordes populating this cosmopolitan city. The place is teeming and she stands out from the muted masses in her striking red and plum ensemble.

Arriving at Mirando Korea headquarters, little notice is paid to Mija. In response, she breaks her way inside – exploding through the glass door into the office. Director Bong describes this moment as the marker of the film kicking into a higher gear: "That's the pistol that goes off and from that moment the pacing totally changes and it goes really fast."

Mija will not stop until Okja is safe and back home.

During her pursuit into the streets and shopping malls of the city, she encounters the Animal Liberation Front, or A.L.F. – they too want to see Okja safe, but they also want to expose Mirando's nefarious schemes, and so their methods will put Okja in even greater danger.

At this point the film begins to broaden in scope and ambition; it's international reach and ensemble cast emerge, showing the film for what it is: a modern-day fable.

At the earliest stages of pre-production, convincing US studios to come on board an original movie of this size proved challenging, as producer Dooho Choi explains: "We met the studios, we met the indie financiers, and it was always about the content – do you really need the slaughterhouse? Do you really need Alfonso? The ones that didn't have a problem with the content – we love your story, we love you – they said this is a $35 million film. It's not $50m+. Either lower the budget or change the content. These were the two categories of response that we got. We had Tilda, Jake, Paul, Steven; Mija was cast already. We had Darius, Kevin, and Erik. We had all these elements. We also had detailed illustrations of Okja and a miniature (maquette) which we showed to financiers. The reality is for us we're just making our film, but I guess for the industry it was just a very strange concept."

Director Bong describes the process straightforwardly as: "Give us fucking money!"

Eventually Netflix came on board, in what would be one of their earliest and biggest original films. They had no issue with the content, the rating, or the cost. "Netflix truly understood what it was and what we needed. It was more the love and respect of the artist that drove them," confirms Choi, "and we appreciate that."

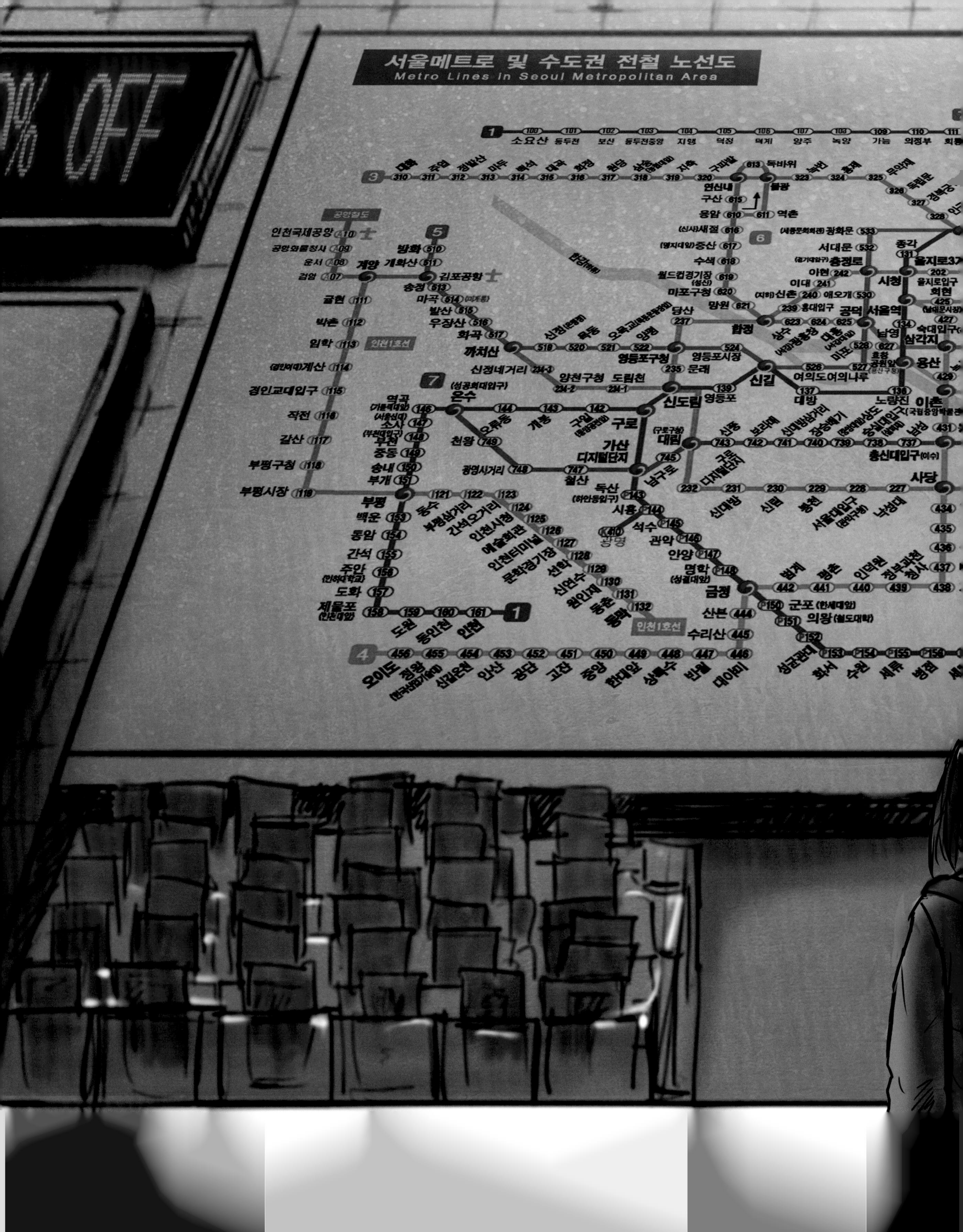
0% OFF
서울메트로 및 수도권 전철 노선도
Metro Lines in Seoul Metropolitan Area

MIRANDO KOREA

RIGHT AND FAR RIGHT: Pre-production imagery of Mija arriving at Mirando Corp. The production design is by Lee Ha Jun.

Mija's only lead is to find Mundo Park (Yoon Je Moon), the Mirando Korea liaison, and hopefully be led to Okja. She is confronted by a long, soulless corridor, a cold front which is offset by the token nod to nature – the tree that forms the company's logo (which ironically turns out to be plastic).

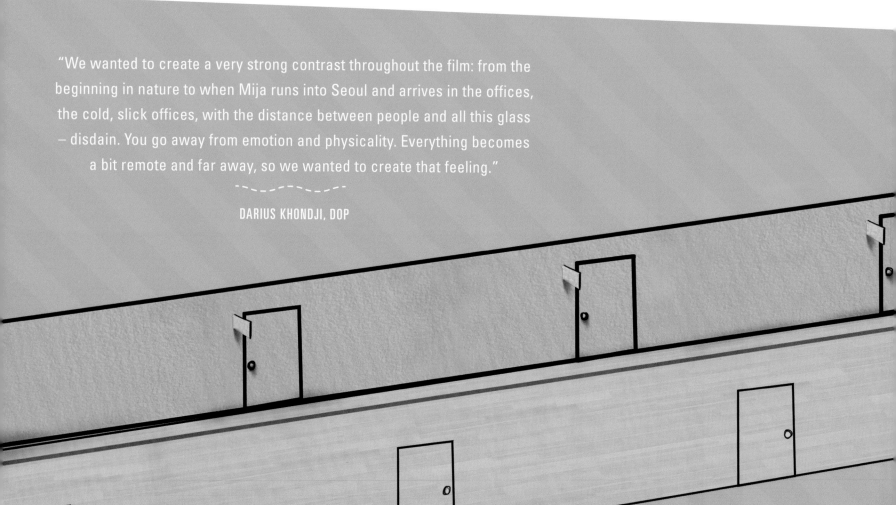

"We wanted to create a very strong contrast throughout the film: from the beginning in nature to when Mija runs into Seoul and arrives in the offices, the cold, slick offices, with the distance between people and all this glass – disdain. You go away from emotion and physicality. Everything becomes a bit remote and far away, so we wanted to create that feeling."

DARIUS KHONDJI, DOP

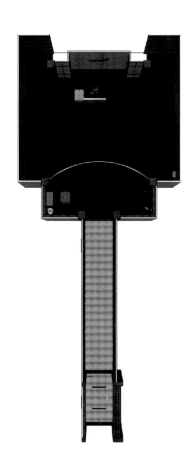

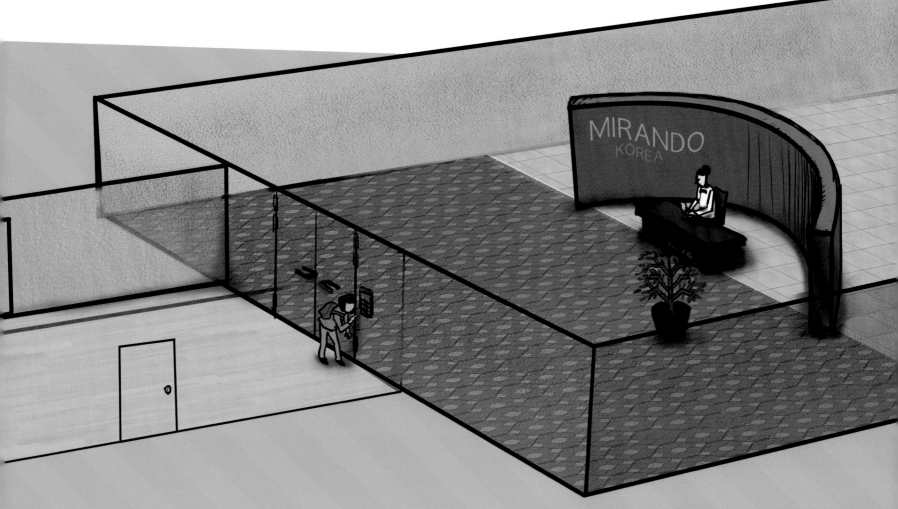

ABOVE AND FAR RIGHT:
Mija searches for Okja inside
and outside Mirando.

RIGHT: Mundo left in Okja's
excrement after the initial
rescue by the A.L.F.

"The theme of the movie is not so much East and West, but more about nature versus urban life. Of course, when Mija and Okja are in the forest, on the farm in the mountain, it's a slower pace. They're in nature. But for me, the marker is when Mija goes to Mirando in Seoul and breaks through the glass."

DIRECTOR BONG JOON HO

THIS SPREAD: Breaking into the Mirando offices, Mija is immediately treated as an intruder with no claim to Okja whatsoever. In the nick of time she sees her friend being loaded onto a truck, eventually to be taken to the USA. From this point on there will be non-stop obstructions keeping the two of them apart, from people to language, or even something as simple as a pane of glass.

Concept art of Okja on the loose and lost, far from home. Every shot containing Okja had to be rigidly planned and prepared for – it is not a question of being able to improvise for VFX-heavy sequences. "The way it was written, the way it was storyboarded, and the way it was planned, that was pretty much how I executed the film," recalls Director Bong. "Especially with VFX films, especially with creature VFX films, because of the complex nature of the work and the sheer cost, you have to make a plan and stick to it. In the very beginning of the process I said I needed about 300 Okja shots and the final shot count is 295. I was pretty much on the mark. Unless you have $100 million, like these VFX movies, you just have to plan and stick to the plan."

RIGHT AND BELOW: Storyboard art showing a fearless Mija leaping onto the truck carrying Okja, which was translated in all its vitality into the shoot. "The tunnel was a complicated one for sure," recalls Darius Khondji. "The chase with the truck, with her running after the truck, jumping on the truck, then the car chase – a challenge."

OPPOSITE TOP AND MIDDLE: Clinging to the roof of the truck, Mija must flatten herself to avoid crashing into the low bridges. This sequence is intercut with the characters in the cabin gauging the height of the bridges themselves – a touch of Director Bong's trademark injection of humor into unexpected moments.

OPPOSITE BOTTOM: A plan describing the truck's route through intercity Seoul.

"When the story starts to fire up and when Mija starts to follow her instinct and her rage to save her friend, she cannot accept that Okja has been taken away to maybe be killed somewhere far away from her."

DARIUS KHONDJI, DOP

"The effects work was really tricky, getting all the extras in the right place looking in the right direction, placing all the cars, switching all that stuff around, dealing with the fumes inside the tunnel, and those incredibly bright lights that gave everybody splitting headaches. It really was a challenging few days, but when you see it in the movie, it's very successful."

ERIK DE BOER, VFX SUPERVISOR

ABOVE: Due to the intervention of the A.L.F., Okja escapes and she and Mija barrel through Seoul and into a shopping mall. The giant pig is loose in the city – circling back to Director Bong's initial daydream that sparked the movie idea.

RIGHT AND FAR RIGHT: Just as they did in the wild, Mija and Okja work together, bounce off one another and always look out for each other. They crash into a gift shop, creating a perfect encapsulation of the movie in a single movement – the collision of consumerism and nature.

ANIMAL
LIBERATION FRONT
JAY – K – RED – BLOND – SILVER

PAUL DANO · STEVEN YEUN · LILY COLLINS · DANIEL HENSHALL · DEVON BOSTICK

"We are animal lovers. We rescue animals from slaughterhouses, zoos, labs. We tear down cages and set them free. This is why we rescued Okja. For forty years our group has liberated animals from places of abuse. We inflict economic damage on those who profit from their misery. We reveal their atrocities to the public. And we never harm anyone — human or non-human. That is our forty year credo."

ABOVE: Blond (Daniel Henshall) takes the lead as the A.L.F. search for Okja in the shopping mall.

RIGHT: Blond and Silver (Devon Bostick) share a couple's embrace of love and comradery.

"The structure is similar to *Snowpiercer*. Each train section, each world, each compartment is very, very different, but basically it's all in the one long train made by the main industrial company at the time. But this time, in *Okja*, they're all from different locations, and barriers create characters, but they're all embraced by the universe of Mirando Corporation. Both films have a lot to say about capitalism."

DIRECTOR BONG JOON HO

RIGHT: The leader of the A.L.F, Jay (Paul Dano), makes their mark on the Mirando truck.

BELOW: Woo Shik Choi plays Kim, the disaffected, disillusioned, soon-to-be-ex Mirando truck driver, and gleeful deliverer of the immortal line: "Mirando is completely fucked!"

THIS PAGE: "For me, the most difficult shots were really the A.L.F. - the initial rescue of Okja by the A.L.F. inside of the traffic tunnel. Opening up the back door of the truck, getting Okja off the truck, then Okja swinging around and reuniting with Mija and coming out of the traffic tunnel, that was a really involved sequence from a shooting point of view. It involved a full Mija double, some greenscreen elements that we shot on the pogo-stick, and then on set it involved at times 5–6 people who needed to be in the right place at the right time pushing or pulling Okja around. We really had to make sure we shot that correctly, because otherwise it would have created too big a puzzle for us to correct in post production." Erik de Boer, VFX supervisor

FAREWELL SEOUL

Through (deliberate) miscommunication, the A.L.F. depart in dramatic fashion by leaping from the truck into the river (the Han River, the same one which the monster in Director Bong's *The Host* emerges from), leaving Mija and Okja to be captured by the authorities and taken into Mirando's custody.

THIS SPREAD: For both major and minor sequences involving CG elements, the visual effects team worked hard to ensure the blend between reality and computer-assisted imagery was seamless. To match the tone, pace, and photography of any given scene, Erik de Boer and his crew would even, where necessary, downgrade the VFX accordingly. "One thing that I've learned on previous projects is that to sell our CGI is our work, and we have to respect the original photography," explains de Boer. "It can be very difficult to work for months on the animation, to render this beautiful asset as 4k resolution, then to put it in the photograph plate only to blur the hell out of it or match live-action elements that arrive beside it. Even if they're in focus but softer, we have to make sure we've got the strongest integration possible."

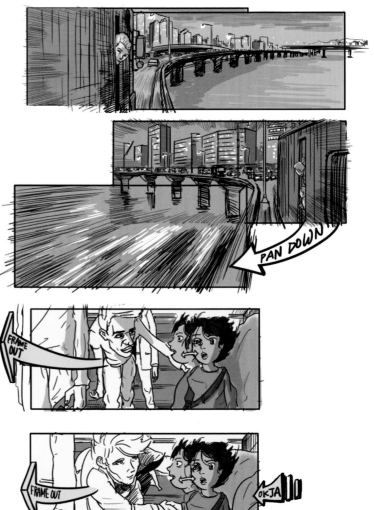

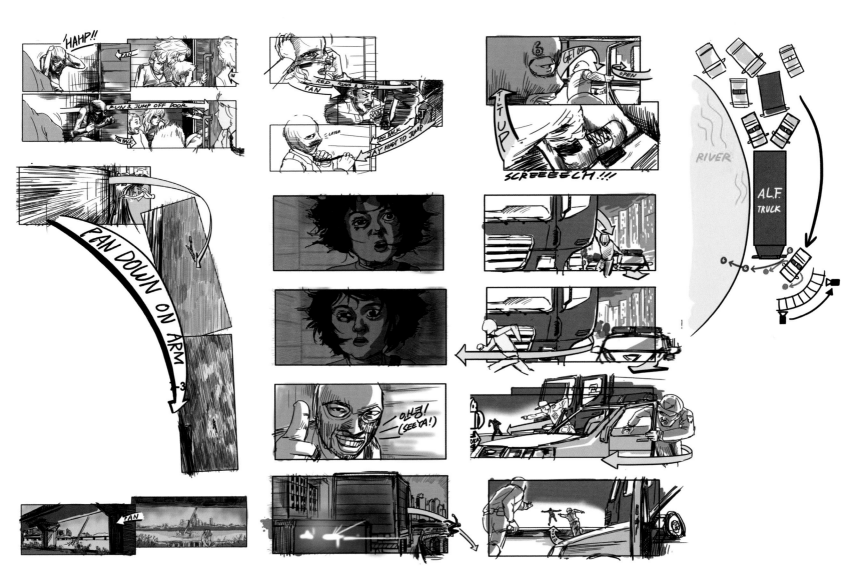

The bridge under which the A.L.F. resurface and reunite is the same one used for the lair of the creature in *The Host*. "Bong wasn't trying to reference that film specifically," clarifies producer Dooho Choi, "he just loves that bridge. Darius made Seoul at night look so gorgeous, but initially the sequence was cut. We later put it back, because it solidifies the A.L.F."

THIS SPREAD: The moment they have been waiting for. As planned, Okja has been taken to the Mirando laboratories and the recording device the A.L.F. planted on her is filming everything. They had presumed the tests conducted on Okja would be harmless... They were wrong.

Steven Yeun (bottom right) plays K, the conflicted conscience of the A.L.F. His loyalty to the cause undermines his ethics, only for him to realise later that "Translations are sacred."

"This set was built in Korea for budgetary reasons, but was designed to look as though it was a low budget motel off the Jersey Turnpike. Details of the motel room were sent from the US to Korea for set dressing needs."

KEVIN THOMPSON, PRODUCTION DESIGNER

ABOVE: Red (Lily Collins) and Silver (Devon Bostick) keep the security guards at bay with their non-fatal weapons.

LEFT: Paul Dano was one of the first actors cast in the movie, having known Director Bong for many years and both eager to find a project to collaborate on.

Jay's trademark black suit, worn throughout the film, is an expression of how seriously he sees his role in the organization and his eagerness for them not to be seen as aggressive radicals.

OPPOSITE PAGE: Jay, K (Steven Yeun), and Silver (Devon Bostick) in and out of typical A.L.F. 'mission' gear.

CHAPTER FIVE

THE LAB

The laboratory where Okja is taken upon landing in the US is the darkest moment in the film for two reasons: the brutal violence Okja is subjected to, and because we finally see where the super pig program originated. It was in a place like this, with its fluorescent lights, dampness, and confinement, where Okja was born.

She is now very far away from her carefree existence in the mountains of South Korea.

By releasing her to Mirando, the A.L.F. counted on exactly this unprecedented access to the Mirando operations. They had presumed that animals were mistreated and exploited, but even they did not anticipate to what degree. As Okja is cattleprodded and dragged in by chains, she sees her kin lining the corridors around her: caged, mutated super pigs, described variously as: "a piglet with a hideously large tumor, one with red, veiny eyes and neck-twitching tic symptoms, one dragging its deformed hind legs…"

The A.L.F. watch the secret transmission with growing unease as a drunk, unstable, maniacal Dr. Johnny first introduces her to the male super pig Alfonso and then to his biopsy gun. Sections of her body are cut from her and given to taste testers, or "half-wit degenerate fucktards". Like the A.L.F., we have been privy to what Okja is going through and now we watch three people eating parts taken from a living thing, a character we have grown to love, without any thought to where it has come from.

ABOVE AND LEFT: Director Bong and Jake Gyllenhaal rehearse the entrance of Okja and review the footage.

OPPOSITE PAGE: Dr. Johnny "Everyone knows I'm an animal lover" Wilcox, fiddles with the app specially designed for Mirando Corporation, an app that when held over a super pig shows exactly how the body will be divided up into which cuts of meat. It's not who a super pig is that matters, it's what it can be used for.

"The lighting is like a metal alloy mixed with very white-green, medical, dim lights overhead, falling on them. Very grim. I just wanted it to feel very horrible, it was a big bit, and I was thinking of Francis Bacon paintings, where there is top light coming down, washing the body. I wanted to get a bit of something like that. It was very queasy."

DARIUS KHONDJI, DOP

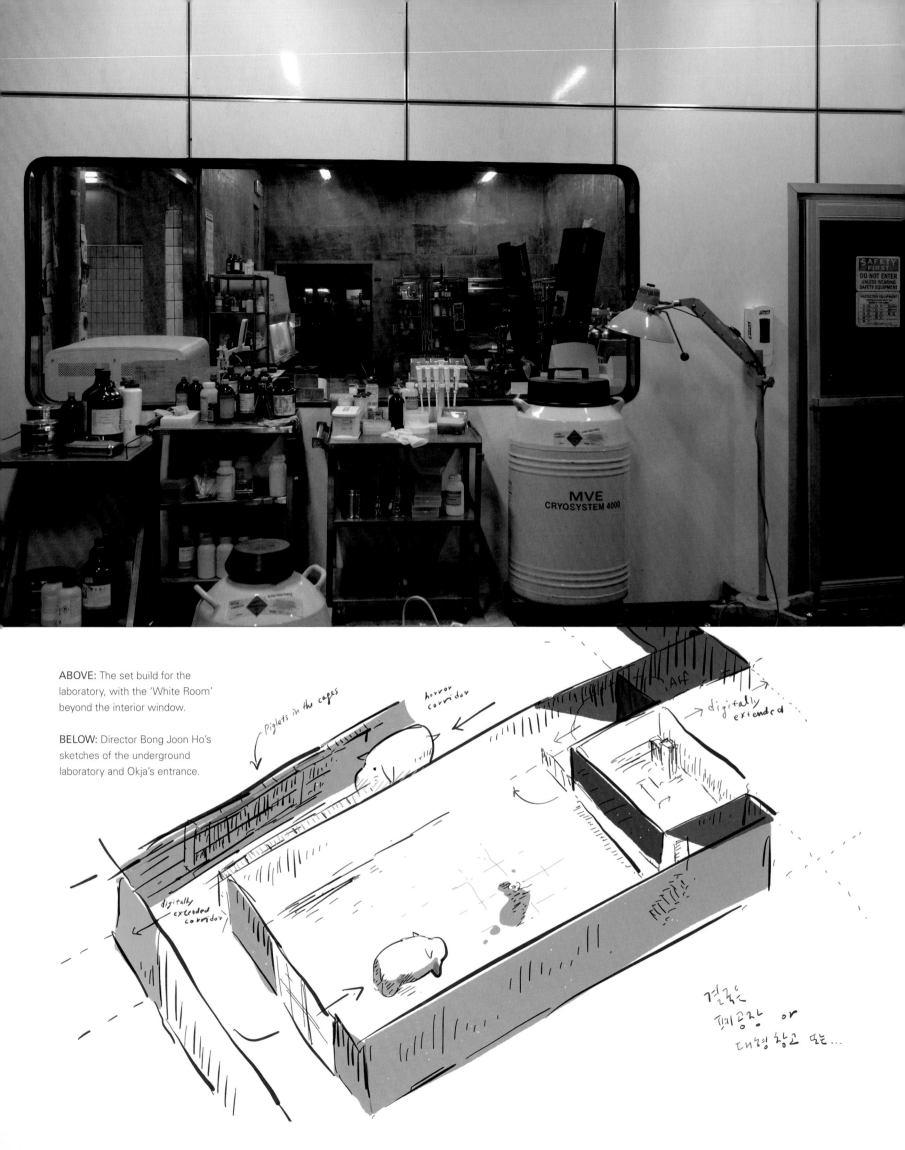

ABOVE: The set build for the laboratory, with the 'White Room' beyond the interior window.

BELOW: Director Bong Joon Ho's sketches of the underground laboratory and Okja's entrance.

RIGHT AND BELOW: Props forming the detritus of the lab set.

BOTTOM: Storyboard by Director Bong, in which Dr. Johnny presents Okja to Alfonso. The placement of the mirror is key, allowing viewers to witness the assault, allowing the A.L.F. to see everything that happens to Okja reflected back at her and them. For both the male and female members of the A.L.F. it is a shameful moment.

> "This is an unspeakable place."
>
> DR. JOHNNY WILCOX

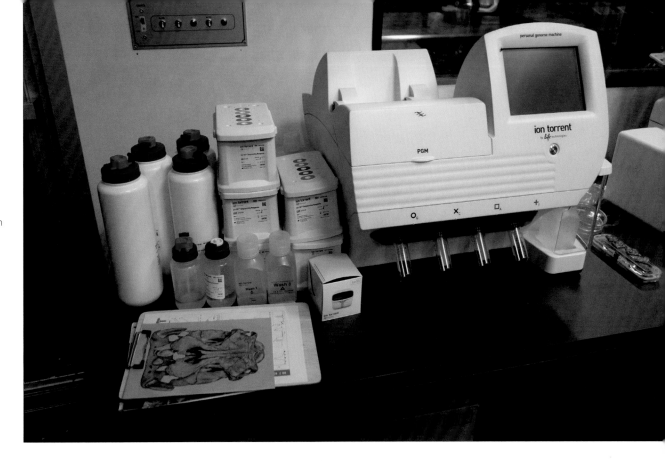

ABOVE: Finished concept art of the harness Okja
is strapped into to make her yield. In the final film
she has a collar and chain - see opposite.

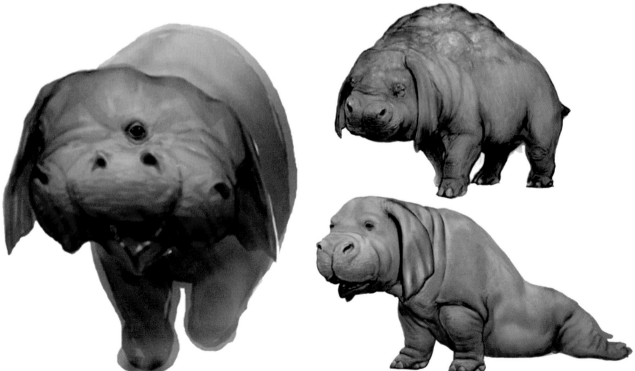

"It's in the underground
laboratory premises in
New Jersey where we
see all these deformed
creatures, the results of
GM experimentation."

DIRECTOR BONG JOON HO

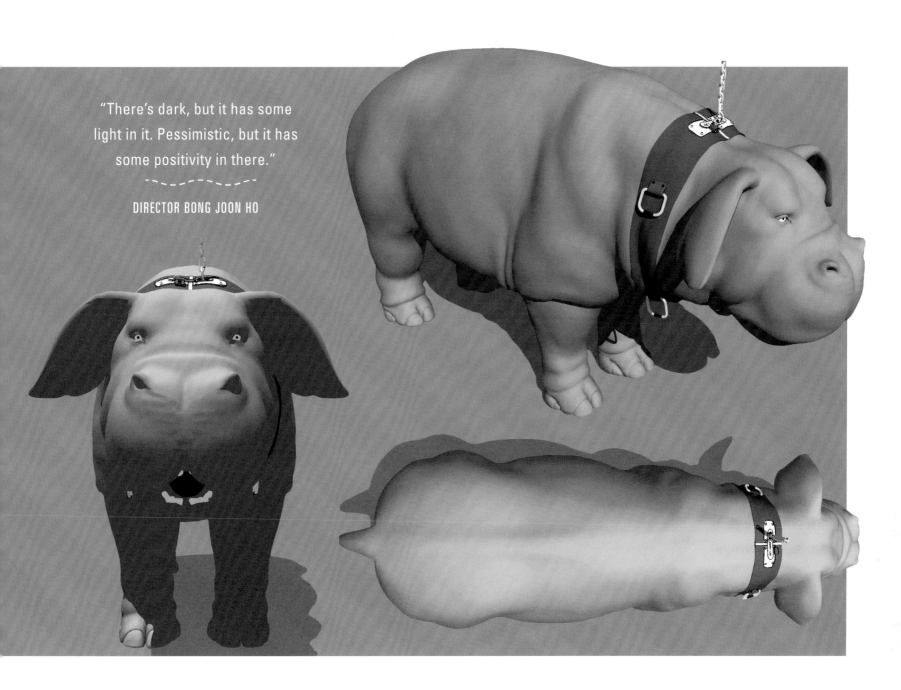

"There's dark, but it has some light in it. Pessimistic, but it has some positivity in there."

DIRECTOR BONG JOON HO

THIS PAGE: Working out the mechanics of Okja's harness through 3D conceptual designs. Restrained against her will, taken from her life in Korea, Okja cannot understand why she was brought to this place.

ALFONSO

"Alfonso is just a penis. The profile when you look at the shape of Alfonso and especially the head area, he's just one giant dick."

DIRECTOR BONG JOON HO

THIS SPREAD: Various Alfonso designs through pen and ink sketches and concept art to CG builds, including one showing Mija present in the scene. In the script Alfonso is described as being 1.5 times as big as Okja.

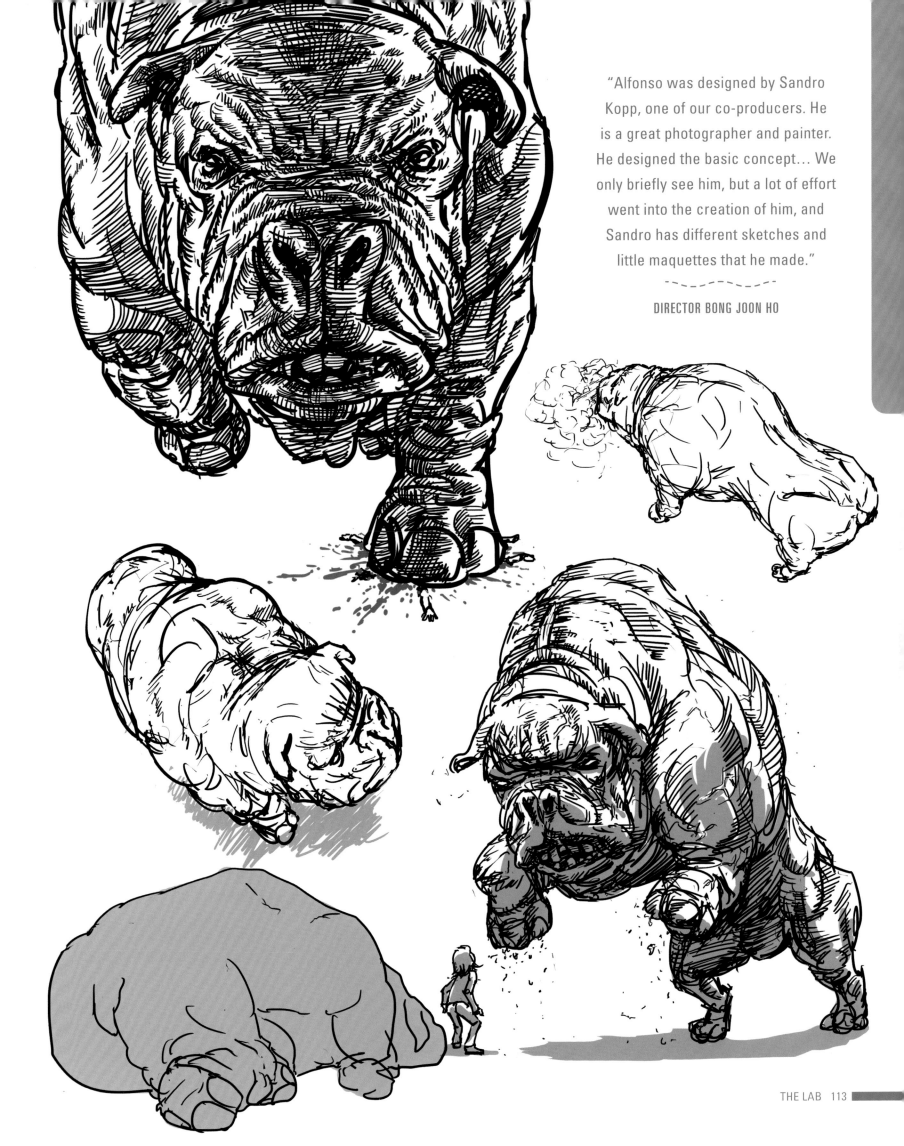

"Alfonso was designed by Sandro Kopp, one of our co-producers. He is a great photographer and painter. He designed the basic concept… We only briefly see him, but a lot of effort went into the creation of him, and Sandro has different sketches and little maquettes that he made."

DIRECTOR BONG JOON HO

CHAPTER SIX

NEW YORK CITY

When the story lands in the US, things become even bleaker. Lucy's grip on Mirando is precarious, Mija is forced into the stereotypical role of a 'wide-eyed ethnic' arriving in glamorous New York City, and Okja is harassed into a place that could not be further from the free and comfortable home she came from.

All points converge in Manhattan, at the climax of the Super Pig Festival. The A.L.F. have plotted to disrupt the parade by publicly broadcasting Mirando's treatment of Okja, and Johnny, Lucy, Mija, and Okja are in the eye of the storm. Meanwhile, Lucy's corporate, cut-throat twin sister, Nancy, watches from the wings.

When the inevitable happens and chaos ensues, Mija attempts to soothe and shield a disoriented and damaged Okja, even protecting her from Jay when he tries to free her from Okja's bite.

The scale of the sequence is enormous, the financial area of Manhattan under siege from protestors, consumers who love the super pig jerky bars, and Mirando's own private security firm Black Chalk. After a brief moment of freedom, Okja is recaptured by Mirando. K, an injured Jay, and Mija make their way to her friend's ultimate destination: the slaughterhouse.

LEFT: Tilda Swinton, reuniting with Director Bong following her role in *Snowpiercer*, was the first actor cast in the film.

RIGHT AND BELOW: In the fallout from the Seoul incident, Lucy and her key advisers (including Frank Dawson played by Giancarlo Esposito and Shirley Henderson as Jennifer) discuss next steps, including bringing Mija to New York and making her a mascot, which means sidelining Dr. Johnny – much to his chagrin.

BOTTOM RIGHT: "My good friend Catherine George – a brilliant costume designer – and I, had a blast with the twins. From early on, we never imagined Lucy in anything other than health clinician-white and kindergarten-pink - a combination of white saviour-goddess, spa-manager, kindergarten teacher, and doll. Flaxen-haired and on a serious mission... she isn't so far away from various Ted-talking – especially health-conscious – 'lifestyle gurus' and entrepreneurs we are aware of."
Tilda Swinton

"I think that [Director Bong] being as precise as he is, having such a fully realised landscape of the film in his head before shooting, means that he is genuinely grateful to performers - and all collaborators - for bringing their energy and contributions to keep him company in building the story. For myself, I fell for his cinema long before I met him, but when we met, we very quickly became friends, inside and outside of making work together. It is this, naturally, that makes cooking things up together so enjoyable for me: to be specific, I think we share a glee in amusing each other which makes for a very light working atmosphere."

TILDA SWINTON

RIGHT: Mija arrives and plays along with Mirando's big moment in order to get to Okja. When eventually the two are (briefly) reunited she finds her friend damaged, all but inconsolable, and looking at the razzle and dazzle of New York through bloodshot eyes.

"I see Lucy as a fool. Damaged and delusional and narcissistic. Her espousing of ethically sound principles is entirely undermined by her cavalier mention of having 'had' to tell 'those little white lies,' while cradling a bouquet in preparation for her great PR triumph. Her interest in the concept of saving the world is primarily an interest in making gazillions of dollars and being popular. Her vanity, fuelled by her toxic competitiveness with her sister, makes her a liar and a cheat. In view of what damage this vanity causes, I wouldn't hesitate to call her villainous: these smiling, dazzling villains are just as dangerous as the grumpy frumpy ones - maybe more so - in that they fool us with their razzmatazz."

TILDA SWINTON

"Paul Dano shows up in the hotel room and has the cards ('We love you,' the whole Dylan reference), then he comes down on the ladder, he changes from the bellboy to a suit, and then rejoins the parade. For me, I've known Paul for about 10 years and it's kind of something you don't see him do in movies now. Just shooting that sequence and just seeing him in that way, it gave me a great thrill; this quiet moment before the storm, that feeling was quite nice to show of Paul."

DIRECTOR BONG JOON HO

DON'T LOOK BACK

뒤쪽을 보지마

SUPER PIG FESTIVAL

KOREA

*empty room with a few abandoned furniture

누군가 어디간 후 비어있는 빌딩의 어느 방. 버리고 간 가구 조금 남아있다.
창문모양 뉴욕 로케이션라 매칭

Shape of the windows should match the ones of NY location's

VANCOUVER

Luxury trailer
Dressing room
Interior set up only
(Nancy & Frank)
낸시&프랭크 고급
트레일러 분장실 내부

VANCOUVER

*upscale restaurant
-Nancy & Frank looking down at the crowd
(낸시&프랭크 시위대 내려다보는 고급 레스토랑)

*B cam-crowd CG plate
(B 카메라-군중 CG 소스촬영)

*window shape matching NOT necessary (창문모양 매칭 필요 없음)

VANCOUVER

Frank

Nancy

MIRANDO

군중 crowd

KOREA

Mirando publicity models toss jerky to the crowd. 군중들에게 비프저키 던져주는 홍보모델들

Marching band
고적대

OKJA

*LED multi-screen interior set up (Blonde)
LED 멀티스크린 내부 (블론트)

"We had several days on Wall Street, which was pretty cool, and what was interesting was that we couldn't really close off that area for tourists or bystanders, so there was a lot of interest and curiosity surrounding that set. Some of those people actually made it into the final movie."

ERIK DE BOER, VFX SUPERVISOR

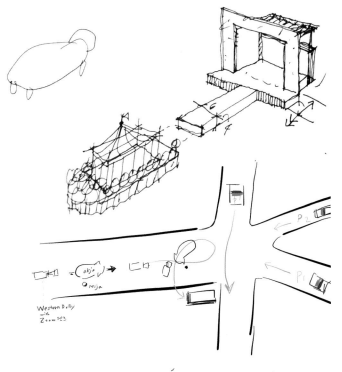

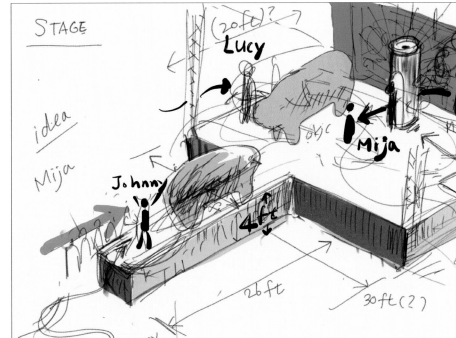

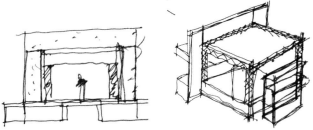

OPPOSITE AND RIGHT: Sketches by Director Bong showing character placement and shooting locations

BELOW: Planning Okja's entrance to the parade, right in the heart of Manhattan.

"Some of the more intricate work that we had to do there with Mija and Okja, that was actually done partially on the sound stage in New York, and partially on the stage in Vancouver, where we shot a few more plates. There's a lot of things that have to come together, directing the extras and costumes, all the props that have to go into that stuff, timing-wise, and then there's us running around with pieces of foam..."

ERIK DE BOER, VFX SUPERVISOR

"It's not that Mija had to be Korean; she could have been Taiwanese or from New Zealand. The idea was to create that contrast: New York City was always where the story ends up and it is the heartbeat of capitalism. We wanted to express how different a world Mija and Okja come from. If you look at the characters, they are all from different places, different worlds, and they all come together because of Mirando, this global multinational biotech company and what it's doing and their interests around the world. It's like a web that connects everybody together, but you would never see Mija unless it was because of this."

DIRECTOR BONG JOON HO

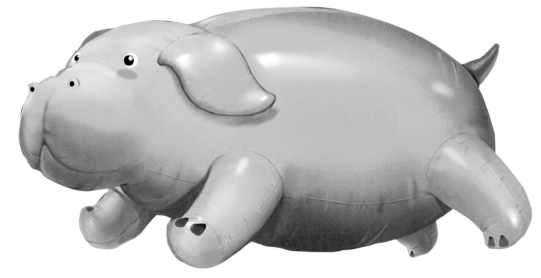

ABOVE: Like the advice given to a heroine in so many fairy tales, Jay tells Mija to not look back. Playing on the screen behind her is the footage of Okja's ordeal in the lab. Mija may not see it, but she can hear it.

RIGHT: Various designs for the Thanksgiving-esque giant inflatable.

OPPOSITE: Storyboarding the festival in full flow, with the crowd eagerly snatching their free bars of super pig jerky.

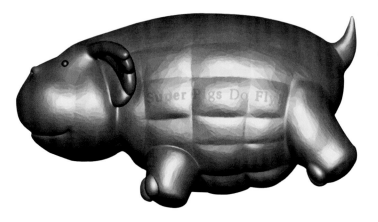

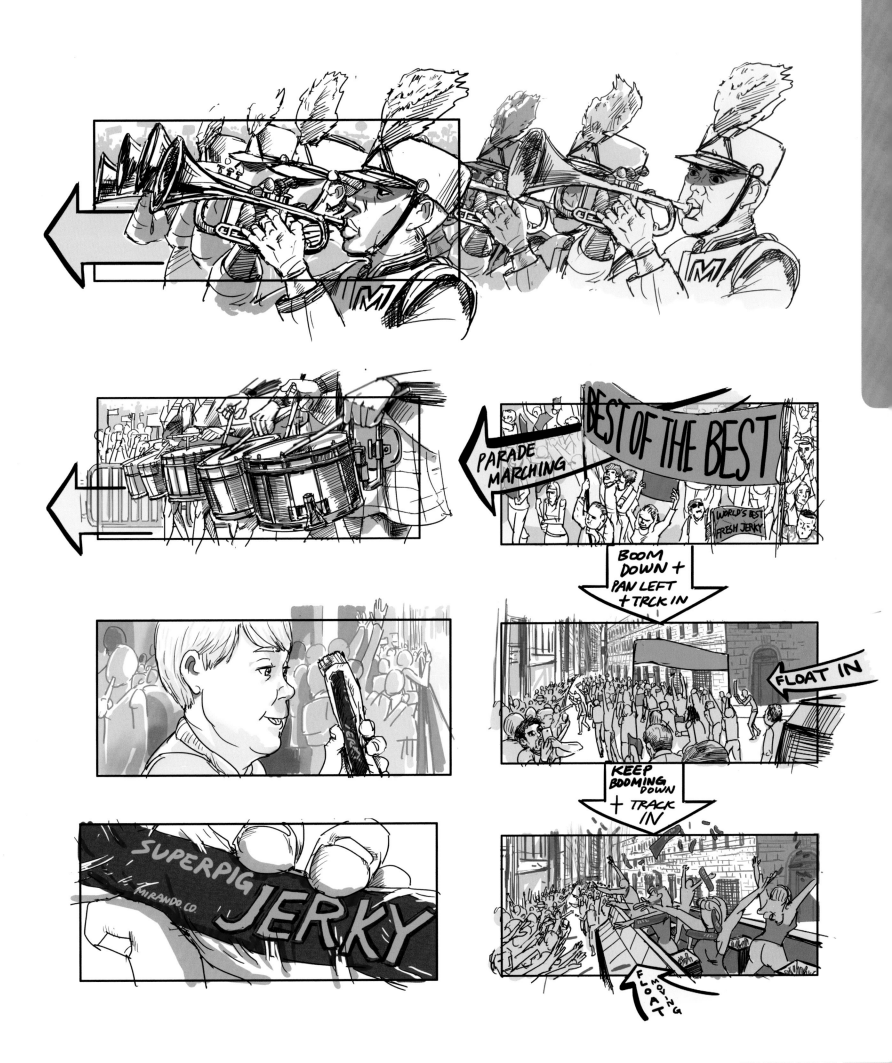

"Jake Gyllenhaal was just mesmerizing to watch play. Paul Dano was amazing. Lily Collins with the red hair. They're just very interesting. They were never a cliché or gimmick, it was more than that, a more humane aspect that you get from a second reading of the characters. I really loved that."

DARIUS KHONDJI, DOP

THIS SPREAD: Storyboard to final film frame comparison of Dr. Johnny's big moment in the spotlight, readying the crowd for Lucy, Mija, Okja, and disaster.

"Specific characters or stories that are parallel to *Okja* are of course *King Kong,* with the narrative drive, being in New York City, and of course George Miller's second *Babe* film, *Pig in the City*. They did a double feature recently in Seoul with *Okja*. I got to see it and had forgotten a couple of details that had inspired me."

DIRECTOR BONG JOON HO

THIS SPREAD: Concept art by Hee Chul Jang illustrating the parade taking place, appropriately, right in the heart of the financial district, with the would-be playful balloons, band, and banners overlooked by the hard corporate structures looming all around.

CHAPTER SEVEN

THE SLAUGHTERHOUSE

The story had to end here. It's as awful as it is inevitable: Okja was created and reared to be eaten, so she is brought to the slaughterhouse. Quite simply, it is her destiny. The feedyard is as nightmarish and as realistic as such a place would have to be. Hundreds of super pigs crammed in pens, an endless line led up the chute to the killing floor. An indifferent worker shoots them in the head and the next one slots into place.

Mija, Jay, and K arrive and the scale of the operation, of the blood, of consumerism, is too much. All they can do is focus on saving Okja – to see if that makes any difference and to see if they can do it before Nancy Mirando arrives.

It was necessary, in a story so full of contrasts and clashes, that Nancy and Lucy are clearly differentiated and opposed, something that required Tilda Swinton to create different approaches for each character. "Interestingly, when she was performing Nancy, it was very natural," is how Director Bong describes Tilda's process. "She was very relaxed. She just took that character and played it. Whereas the scenes with Lucy, for whatever reason, she had a much more sensitive approach. It's interesting to see one actor play two characters and how each character was approached in such a different way. It's just little nuances here in terms of the way things are delivered, but an interesting process to see the same person approach two roles differently."

The characters are having their final showdown in the midst of an emotionally and physically grim place. At this point, almost all the color has been drained from the film, only splashes of blood red remaining. The embrace of nature has been replaced by hard metal lines. To create this 'industrial ground zero' the production inhabited a brewery premises in Canada.

"The whole slaughterhouse shoot happened in Vancouver, which was pretty fun," recalls Erik de Boer. "The brewery is still functional, but it was a part of the brewery that was not being used at the time, so the various departments converted that into a slaughterhouse, with a lot of fake pieces of meat traveling down a conveyor belt where normally beer bottles would be going."

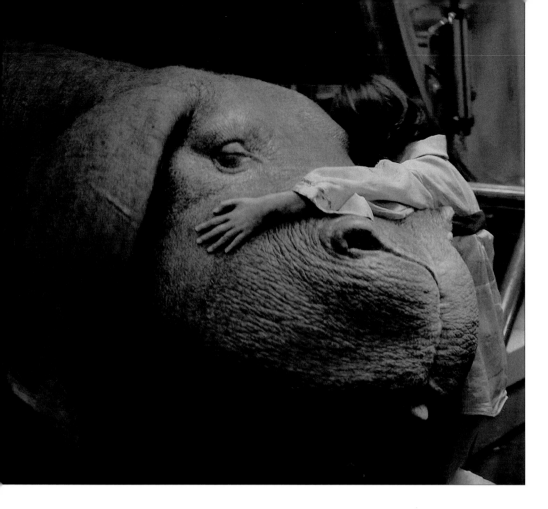

"Lucy and Nancy being twins means we had a chance to imply that Lucy is working hard to remain 'youthful' and dynamic to the point of infantilization, while Nancy has clearly done nothing to disguise her age or present herself in anything other than the most comfortable clothes for golf - she even carries a neck pillow slung round the strap of her handbag. Nancy is strictly a behind-the-scenes kind of despot, puppet-mistress, and delegator of violence."

TILDA SWINTON

ABOVE: This is the very last chance to save Okja. Mija, Jay, and K. infiltrate the slaughterhouse and witness the conveyor belt of death: each super pig pushed up the ramp, held fast, and shot in the head. Then time for the next one.

LEFT: An Seo Hyun, Paul Dano, and Steven Yeun in front of the Alexa 65, shooting at 6.5k, cropped slightly then downgraded to 4k for delivery of the final cut.

ABOVE: Nancy finally removes her sunglasses in order to inspect Mija's offering. The photo of her and Okja did nothing to help her cause, but the golden pig, rolled to Nancy through blood on the hard steel floor, captures the businesswoman's attention.

LEFT: Director Bong working with An Seo Hyun on the climactic scenes.

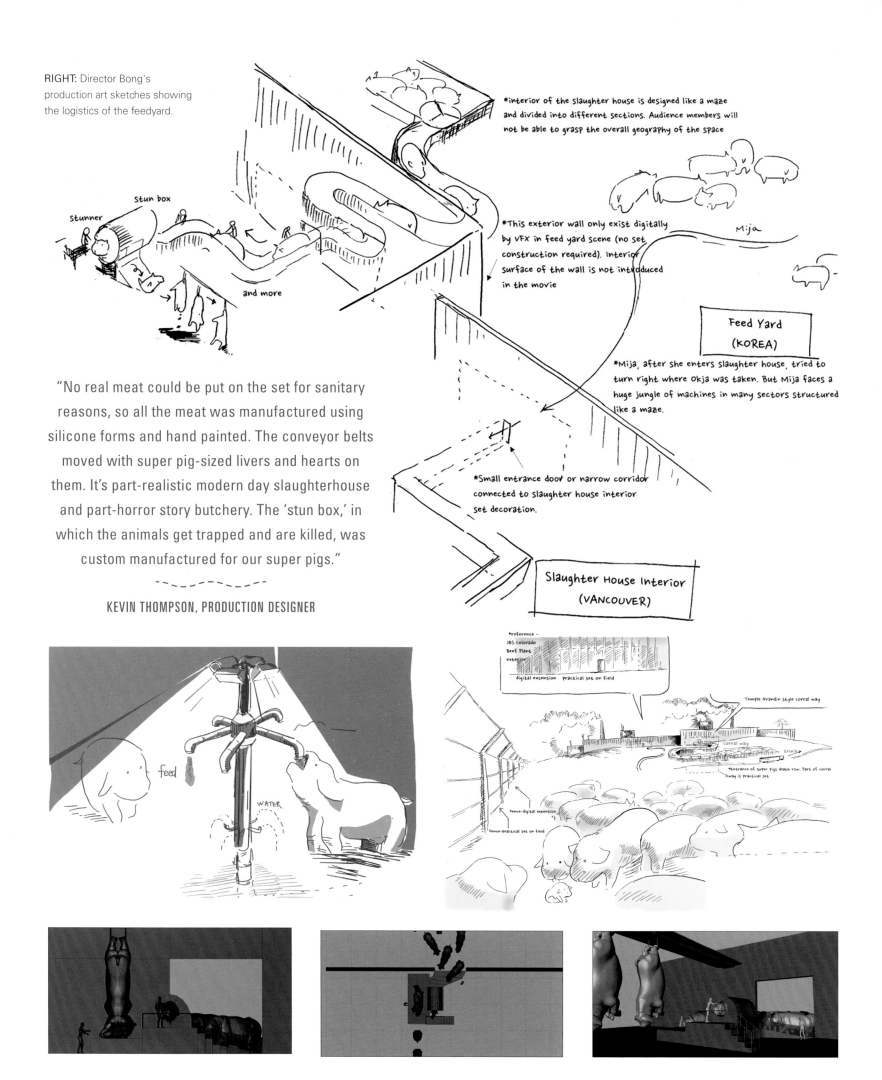

RIGHT: Director Bong's production art sketches showing the logistics of the feedyard.

*interior of the slaughter house is designed like a maze and divided into different sections. Audience members will not be able to grasp the overall geography of the space

stun box

stunner

and more

*This exterior wall only exist digitally by VFX in feed yard scene (no set construction required). Interior surface of the wall is not introduced in the movie

Mija

Feed Yard (KOREA)

*Mija, after she enters slaughter house, tried to turn right where Okja was taken. But Mija faces a huge jungle of machines in many sectors structured like a maze.

"No real meat could be put on the set for sanitary reasons, so all the meat was manufactured using silicone forms and hand painted. The conveyor belts moved with super pig-sized livers and hearts on them. It's part-realistic modern day slaughterhouse and part-horror story butchery. The 'stun box,' in which the animals get trapped and are killed, was custom manufactured for our super pigs."

KEVIN THOMPSON, PRODUCTION DESIGNER

*Small entrance door or narrow corridor connected to slaughter house interior set decoration.

Slaughter House Interior (VANCOUVER)

feed

WATER

*reference - JBS Colorado Beef Plant exterior

digital extension   practical set on field

Temple Grandin style corral way

Corral way

trucks

*Entrance of super pigs death row. Part of corral way is practical set

Fence-digital extension

Fence-practical set on field

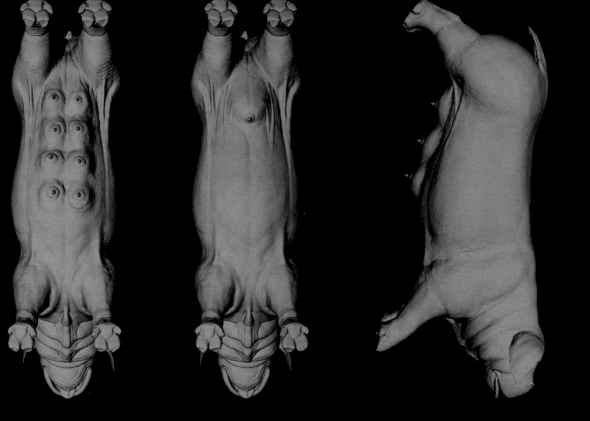

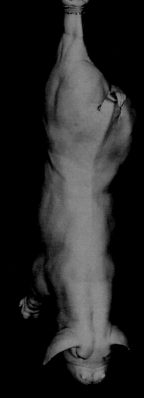

THIS PAGE: "A lot of those sequences were actually shared work with VFX house 4th Creative; inside of the slaughterhouse they did some set extensions where you see some carcasses hanging in the background going off into the distance, and they did that shot of the carcass being sawn in half as well. Then we would take care of all the Okja stuff and the 'hero pig' work, like all the pigs falling out of the box, being shot inside of the box, and that kind of stuff." Erik de Boer, VFX supervisor

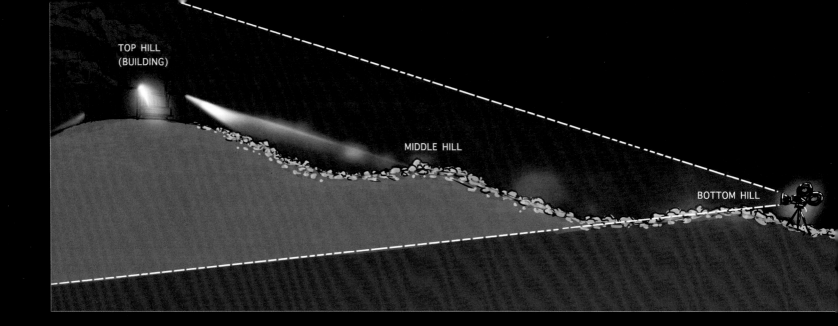

TOP HILL
(BUILDING)

MIDDLE HILL

BOTTOM HILL

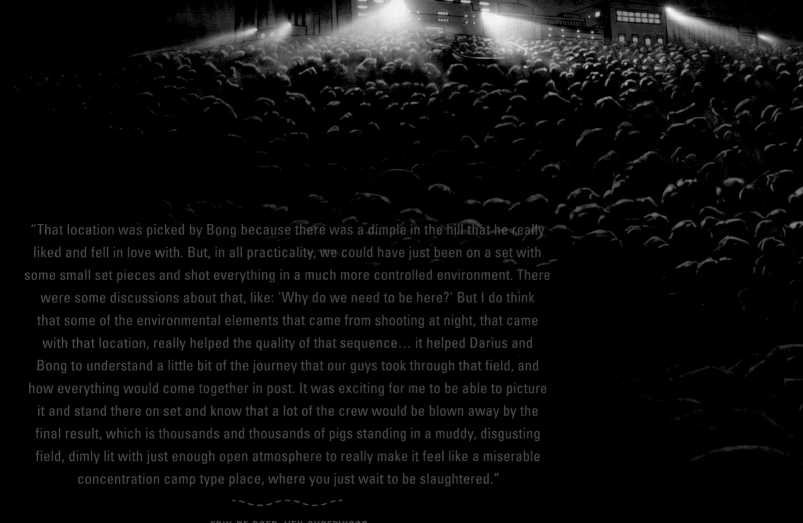

"That location was picked by Bong because there was a dimple in the hill that he really liked and fell in love with. But, in all practicality, we could have just been on a set with some small set pieces and shot everything in a much more controlled environment. There were some discussions about that, like: 'Why do we need to be here?' But I do think that some of the environmental elements that came from shooting at night, that came with that location, really helped the quality of that sequence… it helped Darius and Bong to understand a little bit of the journey that our guys took through that field, and how everything would come together in post. It was exciting for me to be able to picture it and stand there on set and know that a lot of the crew would be blown away by the final result, which is thousands and thousands of pigs standing in a muddy, disgusting field, dimly lit with just enough open atmosphere to really make it feel like a miserable concentration camp type place, where you just wait to be slaughtered."

ERIK DE BOER, VFX SUPERVISOR

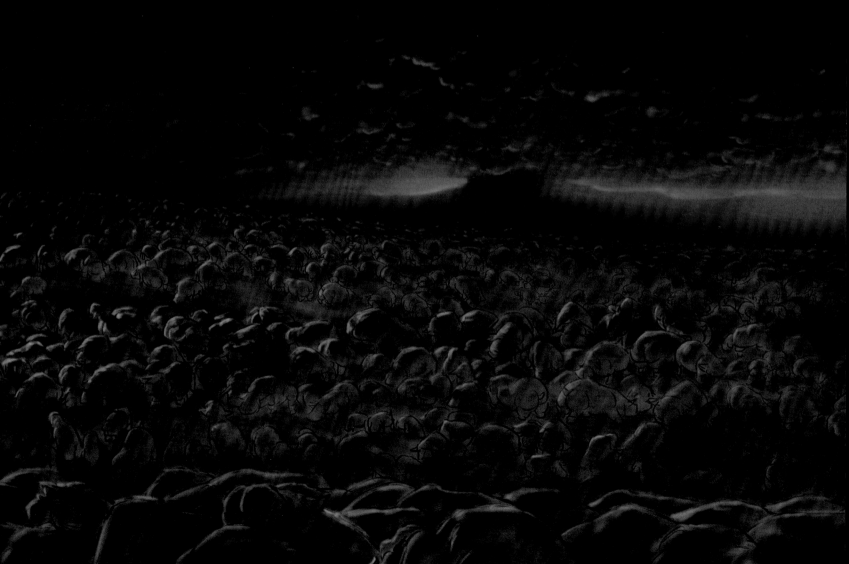

LEFT: "We rigged lights to light the field at night exactly the way it is in the film. The slaughterhouse interior was Canada, but the field exterior was South Korea. When it came to shooting, the actors were lit in this greenish-white light. Everything else didn't exist. The animals going to the slaughterhouse and humans moving among them are all lit realistically, the light bouncing off them in turn, even though the pigs weren't there. Our lighting and the CGI works perfectly together."
Darius Khondji, DOP

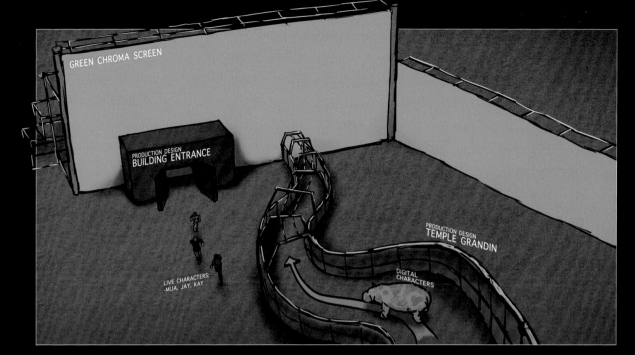

GREEN CHROMA SCREEN

PRODUCTION DESIGN
BUILDING ENTRANCE

PRODUCTION DESIGN
TEMPLE GRANDIN

LIVE CHARACTERS:
-MIJA, JAY, KAY

DIGITAL
CHARACTERS

"Bong had this picture, I think it's probably one of the parks in Zambia, where there's a huge herd of hippos that are standing in the river, and they all have various levels of muck caked onto their skin, some are wet and some of them are dried-out and the light playing over their backs really gave it a very cool graphic pattern. It was important for me to really give it an organic feel and not make it have any hint of CG, or virtual manipulation. I really wanted to make it feel very photographed, so, again, we deteriorated a lot of those areas to make it look as though Darius was there with his camera shooting it."

ERIK DE BOER, VFX SUPERVISOR

PEACE AND TRANQUILITY

Money talks and it is as simple as that. Mija buys Okja and, like that, the nightmare is over. They are transported home, with a super piglet stowaway in tow. The film ends as it began: gently, with the family living peacefully in the South Korean mountains. Equilibrium is restored, but the larger world we have seen and the larger threat of consumerism is unaltered. We must be content with a personal victory.

"I would call it realistic - pragmatic," concludes Tilda Swinton. "Mija and Okja survive their encounter with the capitalistic world, but they are indelibly affected by it. The film is about growing up, becoming conscious, a loss of innocence, maybe. However, Mija and Okja are, perhaps, the exceptions that prove the rule: by refusing to give up on the prevailing truth of real love and not allowing themselves to be beaten down in their determination to return, together, to their life on their mountain, they remain triumphantly consistent spirits, however bruised. This aspect, the possibility of remaining authentic and undivided from one's moral integrity, however close one comes to the source of corruption and exploitation that is the heart of capitalism, is the base note of the film, its soul."

③

소를 정면으로 다가오는 옥자의 큰 얼굴.
뭔가 사람, 어른 같은 눈빛이랄까. 물끄러미 바라보는 미자
입끝이 약간씩 움직이는, 뭔가 속삭이는 옥자 ... 미자가
귀를 들이민다

④ and ⑥
Top

옥자가 미자의 귀에   아주 약간의
뭔가 얘기를 한다.   Track. In.

⑤

옥자가 "Go"   희봉 : 밥 다 식겠다 야!   ④
또는 "가"   ↓ PA
라고 말한다.   ⑥

④ end

미자는,   Piglet이
말을 듣고,   마당의 닭쑥
밥상 쪽으로 ...   여지챙하;

S#105
Shot ⑦

밥상에 와서 앉아 밥을 먹는, 미자.
희봉 와 미자, 말없이 계속 밥먹는 가운데, 뒤로 옥자 다가 오는 모습 보이고 ...
엔드 크레딧 크레디 시작한다:

S#105
Shot ①

텃밭쪽에서 ○○ 를 따가지고 밥상으로 오는 희봉. "어여 와서 밥묵자" "네"
미자와 옥자는 마당을 가리키며 오양간 쪽으로 간다.
새끼돼지가 닭들 사이로 마당을 여지챙한다.

ABOVE: Comparison of Director Bong Joon Ho's own artwork
and the finished stills that bring the movie to its close.

ACKNOWLEDGMENTS

The author would like to thank the following:

My family.

At Titan Books, editorial director Laura Price, designer
Cameron Cornelius, and editorial assistant Ayoola Solarin.

At Netflix, Julie Fontaine, Jennifer Weg, and Collin Creighton.

At Plan B, Christina Oh.

Jason Yu.

And at WME, Tracy Fisher, Eric Zohn, and Jerome Duboz.

For giving up their time and being so insightful and generous,
Darius Khondji, Erik de Boer, Tilda Swinton, and Kevin Thompson.

Finally, and most of all, this book would not have been possible without Director
Bong Joon Ho and Dooho Choi, whose passion and commitment to the idea and
their unique film brought this book to life.

Titan Books and the filmmakers would also like to
thank everyone whose work appears in this book, including:

Storyboard artist: Sung Cho

Still photographers: Jae Hyuk Lee (Korea),
Barry Wetcher (New York), Kimberly French (Vancouver).

Simon Ward is a writer of both fiction and non-fiction and is the author of *The Art and Making of Alien: Covenant, The Art and Making of Kong: Skull Island, Aliens: The Set Photography,* and *The Art and Making of Independence Day: Resurgence.* His essays and articles have appeared in numerous publications, including *Cinema: The Whole Story, 1001 Movies You Must See Before You Die, 1001 Comics You Must Read Before You Die, The Greatest Movies You'll Never See,* and *Sci-Fi Chronicles.* He also wrote the introduction to *Modesty Blaise: The Grim Joker.*